"Sarah!"

In an instant he reached for his daughter, scooped her up in his arms, held her close. "I was so worried...."

Her arms went around his neck, and she buried her face in his shoulder. He hugged her, the little angles of her knees poking him, her tears wetting his shirt. He'd never felt anything so sweet in his life. He had her back. "You're safe now, honey."

Daniel turned to the woman before him. He hadn't seen her on the island before. If he had, he'd have remembered. Short blond hair, sea-green eyes and a splattering of freckles across her cheeks that gave her a sun-kissed glow.

"Thank you." The words were inadequate.

She smiled. "You're welcome."

He held out his hand. "I'm Daniel Gregory, Sarah's father."

Her palm fit nicely into his. "Leigh Christopher."

Daniel knew it was time to thank her again and walk away. But somehow he couldn't just *leave*....

MARTA PERRY

loves seeing the stories in her imagination take shape on the page, so that they can be shared with others. The idea for *A Father's Promise* began in a chance meeting at a church conference with a child whose hearing impairment didn't keep her from doing everything she wanted to do. The Sea Islands, where the author and her husband have a vacation home, provided the perfect setting for the story of Daniel, Leigh and little Sarah.

Marta wanted to be a writer from the moment she encountered Nancy Drew, at about age eight. She didn't see publication of her stories until many years later, when she began writing children's fiction for Sunday school papers while she was a church education director. Although now retired from that position in order to write full-time, she continues to play an active part in her church and loves teaching a lively class of fifth- and sixth-grade Sunday school students.

As is true for Daniel and Leigh, the author has found in her own life that God gives far more than we could ask.

The author lives in rural Pennsylvania with her husband of thirty-six years and has three grown children. She loves to hear from readers and enjoys responding. She can be reached c/o Steeple Hill Books, 300 E. 42nd St., New York, NY 10017.

A Father's Promise
Marta Perry

Love Inspired®

Published by Steeple Hill Books™

STEEPLE HILL BOOKS

ISBN 0-373-87041-8

A FATHER'S PROMISE

Printed in U.S.A.

Now to Him who is able to do immeasurably more than all we can ask or conceive, by the power which is at work within us....
—*Ephesians* 3:20

This book is dedicated to my children,
Lorie, Susan and Scott,
who have taught me much about love.
And, as always, to Brian.

Chapter One

The moment he realized his daughter was lost, Daniel Gregory knew his life had to change.

Alone as usual, he balanced on the second-story beam of what was going to be his oceanfront inn and stared down at the teenage baby-sitter. She stood just outside the construction site, tears streaking her face. He'd feel sorry for her if not for the panic searing his nerves.

"How did this happen?" He swung himself to the sand. "How could you let a deaf child out of your sight?"

"I'm sorry, Mr. Gregory. Honest. I didn't mean to. But the phone rang, and she was just playing on the porch, and I thought I'd only be a minute..."

The girl's excuses ran out, and she gestured up the path to the house.

"You don't think she went toward the water?" Daniel's heart clenched. He shot a glance at the ocean that lapped the shores of the Georgia sea island. The tide was going out; the surf, a gentle ripple.

She shook her head, tears welling. "Sarah's scared of the waves. I don't think she'd go that way. I looked out by the road but didn't see her, so I ran down here to find you."

The girl dissolved in heart-wrenching sobs, and Daniel gave her shoulder a quick pat. He was about as helpless at comforting her as he was at taking care of his child, he thought bitterly.

"Come on, Patsy. We'll find her." He couldn't let the kid see how scared he was, or she'd be no help at all. "You go back up and search the house. I'll check the beach."

Patsy brushed tears from frightened brown eyes. "Right away. I'll look everywhere." She turned and darted up the path through sea grass and palmettos toward the house.

Daniel rounded the edge of the construction, scanning the beach. The usual few tourists, a fisherman or two. No little girl with dark hair in untidy braids and the cords of her hearing aid dangling like a necklace.

He forced himself to look again, tamping down the need to run, to shout her name. Shouting wouldn't do any good. Sarah wouldn't hear him.

His gut cramped. *Sarah, where are you?* If she was on the beach he'd see her, but she could be on any of a dozen paths that led through tangles of scrub growth toward the road. He had to make a choice. He jogged down the beach, his gaze probing every inch of sand and beach grass.

Two months. He'd had his daughter for two short months, and already something bad had happened.

He was the only one in her life she could count on, and he'd let her down.

I promise. Sarah, I promise. I'll find a way to take better care of you. I promise. Just be all right.

"Hurry up, Aunt Leigh. The tide's going out, and I want to look for shells."

Leigh Christopher smiled down at her impatient nephew. Mark had to do everything in a hurry, just like his mother. Her sister, Jamie, always had an agenda in mind, and Jamie's seven-year-old son echoed that quality. Meggie, Mark's five-year-old sister, lagged behind, happily inspecting the tiny insect that crawled along the fan of a palmetto.

"We've got plenty of time, Mark." Leigh shifted an armload of beach towels from one arm to the other.

Mark cast an expert glance at the sun. With his blue eyes and freckles he looked just like Jamie. But Jamie would have been glancing at the businesslike watch she always wore.

"You said you had to go back to the house and work on your...your *résumés.*" He said the unfamiliar word carefully. Mark always had to know the right word for things. "So we have to hurry."

"We're not in that much of a rush," Leigh began, when Meggie tugged at her hand. Leigh turned to her. "What is it, sweetie?"

"Look, Aunt Leigh. Look at that little girl. She's losted."

"Lost," Mark corrected.

"We have to help her." Meggie trotted ahead.

Leigh gazed along the path that wound to the beach. Meggie had seen what Leigh hadn't—a child scrunched against the rough base of a palmetto, arms wrapped protectively around her legs, head down.

Leigh's heart thumped. Meggie was right. She might not know the word, but she knew what *losted* looked like.

Leigh hurried toward the little girl. "Hi, there," she called. "Are you okay?"

The child didn't respond. Meggie scampered up to her and tugged her arm. "Hey, are you losted?"

The little girl jerked up her head at the touch, panic filling eyes that were as dark a brown as her hair. Leigh saw what she wore around her neck, and it hit her like a blow to the heart. A hearing aid. The child was deaf.

It took a moment to recover from the shock, another moment to reach the child. Leigh knelt in the sand, a bramble wrapping around her bare ankle. She snatched off her glasses so the little girl could see her eyes.

"Hi." She smiled, touching her hand lightly. "Are you okay?"

She signed the words as she said them, her mind already busy assessing the child, as efficiently as if she'd never left her classroom. Five or six, maybe. She must have some residual hearing or she wouldn't be wearing an aid.

The child stared at Leigh, her dark eyes frightened. She scooted a little closer to the tree trunk.

Leigh forced herself to sit back. Scared, poor child. Well, of course she was scared, out here alone. Where were her parents? Leigh took a deep breath. *Lord, help me to do the right thing.*

"My name is Leigh." She signed the words

again, finger-spelling her name. Then she added the name sign her first students had given her—an *L* tapped against the dimple that accented her smile. "What's your name?"

Mark tugged at her shoulder. "Why are you signing, Aunt Leigh?"

"Because she can't hear. Or at least, not much." Impossible to tell how much hearing the child had.

"She's deaf? Like the kids you used to teach?"

"Like the kids I used to teach." Her voice wobbled a little on the words, making her angry with herself. That part of her life was over, and it was time to move on.

Meggie leaned around him to pat the little girl's hand. "It's okay. We're friends." Slowly she finger-spelled her name, the way Leigh had taught her. "Meggie. I'm Meggie."

For an instant the child's ability to respond hung in the balance. Then, with the smallest of gestures, the child's fingers began to move. *S-A-R-A-H.*

"Sarah." Leigh let her breath out in relief. Now they were getting somewhere. At least the child—Sarah—understood them. That should take some of the fear away.

"I'm Leigh," she said again. "This is Mark..." She finger-spelled the name. "And Meggie."

Sarah ducked her head shyly. She must not have been around other children much, judging by the fascinated way she stared at Leigh's niece and nephew. Why not? She was certainly old enough to be in school.

"How old are you, Sarah?"

She was ready to ask again, when Sarah held up her hand, spreading five fingers wide.

"Five!" Meggie exclaimed, grinning. She tapped her chest and nodded. "Me, too."

Sarah smiled back. Meggie might not know much signing, but she was doing a better job of communicating with Sarah than Leigh was. Leigh captured the child's attention and signed as she spoke slowly.

"Who did you come to the beach with today, Sarah? Was it Mommy?"

The little face froze, and then she shook her head violently, braids and hearing-aid cords flopping.

Something about her innocent question had upset the child. She hated to push, but she had to get some answers in order to help.

"Daddy?" she questioned.

Sarah nodded vigorously. "Dad—dy," she pronounced, speaking for the first time.

"Nice talking, Sarah." The words came out of Leigh's mouth automatically, her standard response when one of her students attempted to verbalize. It *was* nice talking, especially in this case.

"Where is Daddy?"

The brown eyes filled suddenly with tears, piercing Leigh's heart. She longed to hold the little body close and comforting, but she didn't want to risk scaring her further.

Meggie wasn't held back by that concern. She shoved her way past Leigh and put both arms around Sarah.

"It's okay." She patted Sarah as if the child were one of her many dolls. "It's okay. We'll find your daddy."

Of course they'd find him. But where was he? Leigh looked toward the beach, then back along the path toward the road. Nothing. The parents of children with disabilities were usually overprotective to a fault in her experience, especially fathers. How had Sarah's father been so careless as to lose her?

She stood, trying to decide the best thing to do. She could take Sarah to the island police station, but she hated to put her through that if it wasn't necessary.

"Tell you what." She held out her hand to Sarah, giving her an encouraging smile. "Let's walk down to the beach. Maybe we can find Daddy."

And if not, they could walk back up to the nearest phone and call for help. There had to be one closer than her sister's place.

Sarah stared at Leigh for a long moment. Then she got up, dusted sand from her shorts and took her hand.

Leigh's fingers closed around the small hand, and her throat tightened. She managed a smile. "Let's go."

He had to turn back, had to run for a phone and set a search in motion— Then Daniel saw them coming toward him down the path. A woman, a couple of towheaded kids and his Sarah.

"Sarah!" In an instant he had reached her, scooped her up in his arms, held her close. "Sarah, I was so worried."

Her arms went around his neck, and she buried her face in his shoulder. He hugged her, the little angles of her knees poking him, her tears wetting his shirt.

He'd never felt anything so sweet in his life. He had her back. If he had to wipe out everything he'd saved to hire a decent sitter, he'd do it. This was never going to happen again.

Carefully he peeled away the stranglehold Sarah had on him so he could see her face. "Honey, it's okay. You're safe now."

The smallest of smiles peeked out from behind the tears, like sunlight through the clouds.

He smoothed tangled dark hair back from her face, coaxing a bigger smile. "Okay? That's my girl."

She nodded, brushing away tears with the back of her hand.

Tugging his attention from Sarah, he turned to the woman and kids. The two little towheads looked familiar—Josh and Jamie Reynolds's kids, he thought they were. But the woman...

He hadn't seen her on the island before; Daniel knew that. If he had, he'd remember.

Slim, straight, almost tomboyish in jeans shorts and a T-shirt, except that no boy sported curves like that. Short blond hair ruffled by the wind; sea-green eyes; a spattering of freckles across her cheeks, giving her a sun-kissed golden glow. She reminded him of a buttercup, all yellow and windblown.

"Thank you." The words were inadequate.

She smiled, and a misplaced dimple appeared at the corner of lips that curved upward easily. "You're welcome. I know how scary it is to lose one of these creatures." She gestured toward the two Reynolds kids.

He shifted Sarah to his left shoulder so that he could hold out his hand. "I'm Daniel Gregory. Sarah's father."

Her palm was warm and a little sandy, and it fit nicely into his. "Leigh Christopher."

His fingers tightened a little. "Nice to meet you, Leigh. And thank you again." To his embarrassment, his voice roughened on the words.

"Our pleasure."

Time to end the exchange and walk away. Somehow he didn't want to do that.

"Are you the Reynolds's baby-sitter?"

"No—" she began, but the little girl preempted her.

"She can't be our baby-sitter!" For some reason she seemed to find that hilarious. "She's our aunt!"

The boy frowned at his sister. "Stupid, she could still be our baby-sitter, if she wanted to be, but she's not. Aunt Leigh teaches deaf kids—" He stopped suddenly, a blush sweeping across his freckled face.

"It's okay." Leigh tousled his hair. "Mr. Gregory knows Sarah is deaf."

"'Daniel,'" he said. "Not 'Mr. Gregory.'" He liked her easy manner with the kids. Liked everything he'd seen, in fact. He found himself wanting to see that generous smile again.

"I know Josh doesn't have any sisters, so you must be Jamie's. Are you visiting long?"

"Probably the rest of the summer." She touched the two kids. "Have to spend some time with these guys before they grow up on me."

"Aunt Leigh's looking for a new job," the boy informed him. "She sends out résumés every day."

Now it was her turn to blush, and she met his eyes with a rueful smile. "No privacy around kids, is there?"

"Not much privacy on an island anyway." His mind churned, way too fast. He had to think this through, but he couldn't let her get away. Maybe, for once in his life, the answer to his problems had dropped right into his lap.

"Look, I need to get Sarah back to the house, but I'd like to talk to you again. Are you going to be on the beach for a while?"

He thought he saw something a little wary in those sea-green eyes, but she nodded. "We plan to do some serious beachcombing today."

"Good." He cradled Sarah against him. "I'll see you a little later, then."

She nodded, then touched Sarah lightly, signing as she spoke. "Goodbye, Sarah. I'm glad we met you."

His shy daughter smiled in return, then waved to them. He realized she was trying to finger-spell Leigh's name.

Daniel's heart beat somewhere up in his throat. That was more than she'd tried to communicate with anyone else in the two months since she'd come to live with him. Leigh Christopher was the perfect answer to his problems. And all he had to do was figure out how to convince her of that.

"Aunt Leigh!" Mark tugged her hand. "Don't you want to help us finish the sand castle?"

Leigh pulled her gaze from the retreating waves and suppressed a yawn. "Sure I do." She knelt beside him. "Wow, what a great job. How about a moat?"

Meggie ran to fill her green plastic bucket with water, and Mark began burrowing out a trench.

Leigh dug her fingers through hot surface sand to the cool moistness beneath, watching Meggie fill her bucket, spill it, then patiently approach the next wave. Too many more sun-drenched, lazy days like this and she'd turn into a vegetable.

Well, that was the idea, wasn't it? She'd come to St. Joseph's Island for just that reason, and in the short time she'd been here, she'd already begun to heal. The encounter with Sarah had been distressing, but the memory of the upheaval receded, slipping away like the tide ruffling the sand, then smoothing it out.

Meggie ran back, water slopping from the pail and splashing her bare brown legs. She sent a convoy of sandpipers veering in another direction as she sloshed to a stop.

"Wait, wait," Mark directed, his voice fussy. "I haven't finished the moat yet. You and Aunt Leigh have to wait until I'm done."

Meggie looked ready to argue, but Leigh was perfectly happy to lean back on her elbows and watch him work. Peace flooded over her, a peace she hadn't experienced in months. Yes, a few more days like this...

A shadow fell across the sand castle. Leigh looked up, shading her eyes with her hand, but somehow she already knew whom she'd see. Eyes like bittersweet chocolate, dark hair cut short with a ruthless hand, a lean face and a determined jaw. Daniel Gregory.

"Mr. Gregory!" Mark grinned at him. "Look at my castle."

"Our castle," Meggie said. "Mine, too."

"It's great." Daniel squatted next to Leigh. He

patted a little extra sand into place on the castle wall with one strong hand and smiled at the children. "You did a fine job."

"Does your little girl like to build sand castles?" Meggie, always ready to be friends with the world, leaned confidingly against his knee.

Daniel frowned, sending a glance toward Leigh that she couldn't understand, and a flicker of uneasiness went through her.

"Sarah doesn't like playing on the beach much."

"She'd like it if she played with me," Meggie said, confident in her ability. "Bring her to play with me."

Daniel was beginning to look a bit overwhelmed by Meggie's volubility. Maybe she'd better rescue him. She handed Meggie an empty pail.

"We need more water for the moat. Why don't you go and get some."

Meggie ran off, and Leigh smiled at him. "The rescue is on the house. She loves to talk."

He met her smile with an intent look in those chocolate brown eyes. "I wish Sarah did."

"I know," she said softly. That was always a problem. Hearing parents hoped against hope that their children would learn to speak. Some even refused to sign, as if denying the situation would make it go away.

Daniel squared his body toward her. He was close enough that she could feel the heat that radiated from his olive skin. "I want to talk to you."

Leigh shrugged, feeling ridiculously off balance. "We are talking, aren't we?" All right, he was an attractive man. Very attractive. That was no reason for her breath to quicken or her pulse to suddenly beat a tattoo in her throat.

Brown eyes locked on hers, holding her gaze captive.

"It's about something important. About my daughter. Sarah."

His voice softened on the name, and something melted inside her. She'd always been a fool for that kind of gentleness in a strong, rugged man.

"Sarah's a darling," she said.

"Sarah needs help," he countered.

Trouble, that's all she could think. Whatever he wanted, it meant trouble. She glanced at Mark, but he'd moved away to dig up some fresh sand, and Meggie splashed through an inch or two of water, trying to scoop it up.

Leigh leaned back, as if an added inch of space between her and Gregory might give her an advantage.

"Look, I know you don't know me." He frowned. "I know this is sudden. But your brother-in-law can vouch for me, and I can get references...."

"What are you talking about?" She knew what was coming now, and the peace of the day unraveled in an instant.

"I want you to work for me, taking care of Sarah."

He said it in a rush, as if he had to get the words out in a hurry. As if asking anyone for help were a blow to his pride.

"I'm not looking for a job," she said quickly.

"But Mark said you were filling out résumés."

She felt her cheeks warm. "I know. I mean, I'm

not looking for that kind of a job.'' Not ever again. ''And anyway, you don't know anything about me.''

He smiled, as if the hard part were over. As if convincing her to agree to what he wanted would be a piece of cake. ''I know you're Jamie Reynolds's sister. I know they trust you with their kids. I know you're a teacher of deaf children.''

''That doesn't mean I'm the right person for Sarah.'' She had to think. She wasn't about to take on this challenge, and she certainly wasn't about to tell him why she would never again be teaching.

His hand came down over hers suddenly. His palm, roughened by hard work, set her skin tingling.

''I also know you're warm and generous with kids, and they like you instinctively. And I know Sarah talked more to you in five minutes than she's talked to anyone else in the two months she's been here.''

She took a breath, let it out, then drew her hand away as Meggie splashed back up with her pail. Two months? Where had Sarah been before she'd come to the island?

''Sarah's mother...'' she began, then stopped, not sure she should ask the question.

''She died in an accident.''

A protective barrier screened his eyes, warning her away.

''Sarah is living with me now. And I want the best for her.''

A hundred questions bubbled up in Leigh, but she couldn't ask them. Not of him, not now. Not when he was obviously dealing with a great deal of pain.

Not when she had no intention of doing what he wanted.

"I'm sorry. Of course you want the best for Sarah, but I'm really not looking for that kind of a job. I've been filling out résumés because I hope to find something in another field by the end of the summer."

"You're leaving teaching?"

The question was like a knife to her heart. "Yes." She could only hope the monosyllable would discourage any questions. She glanced at Mark and Meggie, who were sitting back on their heels, listening wide-eyed.

He looked down at the sand castle for a moment, his hand absently patting at its towers. Then he looked back at her. "That wouldn't be a problem. If everything goes the way I plan, Sarah will be attending a residential school in the fall. Right now is when I need someone. You could still go for interviews, if that's what's worrying you."

Residential school... Her mind brimmed with objections that were none of her business. Since she had no intention of doing as he asked, she couldn't interfere.

Doing as he asked. For a moment her treacherous mind toyed with the possibility of her working with Sarah, of her teaching again. She pictured that solemn little face smiling, communicating. She saw herself tapping into the energy and intelligence that hid behind Sarah's deafness.

No. It was impossible, and even considering it would be opening herself up to the kind of emotional pain she had barely started to recover from.

Not to mention the totally inappropriate sizzle she felt when she was near Daniel Gregory.

"Look, I just can't." She forced her voice to be cool and firm. "I'm sorry, but it's out of the question." She stood. "Come on, kids, we've got to get home. Gather things up now."

Daniel stood when she did, still way too close. When she moved, his hand closed lightly on her wrist. The slightest movement would break the contact, but she didn't move.

"Think about it." He leaned closer, a breath away. "Think about it. We'll talk again."

Chapter Two

"Well? Get what you wanted?" Joe Phillips leaned on the registration desk in the ramshackle old house that was part home, part fishing lodge, his elderly face as weathered as the frame building. He'd come with the lodge when Daniel bought it and had long ago decided that fact gave him the right to know everything that Daniel did. He was the closest thing to family Daniel had, and it was good to have someone who was concerned about what happened to him and Sarah.

Daniel glanced at his daughter, watched as she put her doll to sleep in its cradle in the corner, apparently none the worse for her adventure.

"Not yet." He took the glass of lemonade the other man held out to him. "But I will."

Joe wrinkled his nose at that. "Don't always get what we want. Not in this life."

He stared down at the registration book, as if fascinated by the story it had to tell. Daniel knew what he was seeing only too well—there were eight rooms in the old lodge, but only three of them were occupied at the moment.

"I will this time." Daniel drained the glass. The tangy liquid rinsed the salt taste from his lips. "I'll get Leigh Christopher to watch Sarah, and we'll get the construction finished. By the time the new bridge opens, we'll be ready for the tourists." He set down the glass and reached across the counter to straighten the bow tie Joe insisted on wearing when he worked. "We're going to be rich, old man." He glanced at Sarah. "Rich enough, anyway."

Joe readjusted the tie to his satisfaction. "Don't see how you can make the lady teach Sarah if she says no. Woman's made up her mind. It's like telling the tide not to come in."

Daniel smiled, feeling confident for the first time in a long time. "This was meant to be."

"Then why didn't she say yes right away? Sounds like she knows her own mind."

"Maybe I came on a little too strong today." Daniel shrugged. "I'll go over there tonight, apologize, ask her to help me out, just for a couple of days."

Sarah was putting the doll to bed again, an endless repetition of the same action...patting it, snuggling it, loving it. He'd given up trying to figure out what it meant, but it broke his heart all the same.

"Once she's been around Sarah for a couple of days, she'll see how much Sarah needs her. She won't be able to let her down."

The way I did. The way Ashley did. The way everybody in her short life has done.

The only thing, the only person he or Sarah could rely on, was him. Not other people, not God. He should have learned that lesson by now.

He frowned out the window at the skeleton of the addition he was building to the inn. Sarah's future. That was her security, and this time he wouldn't let her down.

As for Leigh Christopher—something about that generous smile and tender touch told him she wanted to agree. So what was holding her back?

He puzzled at it, trying to imagine a scenario to explain the woman's actions. Finally he shook his head.

It didn't matter. It didn't matter what her reason was, because he wouldn't give up until she said yes.

"We're home," Leigh called. She shook out the sandy beach towels and spread them on the gray deck rail. Josh and Jamie's cedar shingle house nestled under the live oaks at the edge of the salt marsh, and the deck overlooked its constant changes as the tide pushed up the creek into the marsh, then receded.

"Home and hungry, I'll bet." Jamie held the kitchen screen door wide, welcoming her children with hugs. She wrinkled her nose at Meggie's salty, sandy bathing suit. "You two get out of your swimsuits and wash up. And don't forget to rinse out those suits. Supper will be on the table in a little while."

Of course it would. Leigh looked at her sister, her affection mixed with both awe and amusement. Jamie had worked a full day at her accounting business and she'd still managed to beat them home and have supper cooking when they came through the door. High achiever had always been Jamie's middle name.

"We found a losted little girl," Meggie informed her mother. "And she couldn't hear, so I spelled my name like Aunt Leigh showed me."

"Lost," Mark corrected his little sister for the tenth or eleventh time. "She was lost and she was deaf. So Aunt Leigh talked to her and then she found her daddy. We helped."

"And her daddy wanted Aunt Leigh to come work for him, but she wouldn't." Meggie turned that direct blue gaze on Leigh. "Why wouldn't you, Aunt Leigh? You could bring her here and we'd play."

"Because I have other plans, pumpkin." Leigh gave her talkative niece a hug.

"But it would be fun," Meggie protested.

Leigh ruffled her hair. "Didn't I hear Mommy say something about getting washed up? Hurry, and maybe we'll have time for a game."

"Chutes and Ladders!" Meggie shouted. "I'll get it."

"Wash first," Jamie said.

"We will, Mommy." Mark raced Meggie down the hall.

Jamie turned to Leigh, her blue gaze just as direct and inquiring as Meggie's. Only, she was a lot harder to deflect than Meggie. Leigh's heart sank. Jamie would not understand this decision.

"Think I'll take a shower before the game," she murmured.

Jamie raised an eyebrow. "A deaf little girl. That must be Daniel Gregory's child."

"Now, how did you— That's right, he said he knew you and Josh." Leigh took a step toward the door, hoping to escape a discussion.

Jamie moved in front of her. "Come on, tell all."

"It was nothing, Jamie." Leigh suspected her sibling wouldn't be convinced.

Jamie gave her a big-sisterly look. "Right. Now, tell it fast, before the monsters get back and drag you into that game you rashly promised." She cast an affectionate glance toward the hall.

Leigh shrugged. Trying to evade her sister had always been worse than useless, whether she was playing tag or keeping a secret.

"You already heard it from the town criers. We found her, we restored her to her father, end of story."

"Aren't you leaving something out? How about the part where he asked you to work for him?"

"He's looking for someone to take care of Sarah. I told him I wasn't interested."

Jamie gave Leigh her accountant look, as if Leigh were a doubtful number in a column of figures. "Not interested? Leigh, it's a chance to work with a deaf child again. How could you not be interested?"

"I'm not going to do that any more, Jamie. Remember?"

Jamie's mouth set stubbornly. "Well, it would certainly be a lot better than waitressing all summer while you look for a new job."

"Jamie..." Familiar frustration welled in Leigh. She loved her sister dearly, but this disagreement was getting old. "Just leave it alone, okay?"

Her sister's blue eyes looked as stubborn as
Mark's.

"I know it's been difficult, but you've got to put
it behind you."

"I can't." The lump in Leigh's throat was big
enough to choke a horse.

"If you'd just try harder..."

Leigh shook her head. Jamie loved her, but she
didn't understand. "Please don't bug me about this.
I'm sorry for Daniel and Sarah, but I can't get involved. I can't do it."

"So you're going to throw away your training
and go into some other field entirely."

"Lots of people change jobs. It's practically a
national sport."

"Not for someone like you. You have a precious,
God-given gift. You can't turn your back on it."

A God-given gift. Was that really what Jamie
thought her abilities with deaf children were? If so,
it had turned into something closer to a curse.

"I have to do this my own way." She tried to
smile. "This time, big sister, you can't make it all
better, no matter how much you want to."

Jamie studied her, looking as if she considered a
whole series of arguments. But finally she nodded.
She patted Leigh as if she were one of the children.

"All right. I won't bug you about it any more
now."

Leigh started to turn away, but Jamie caught her
hand.

"Just...pray about it, Leigh. Will you?"

Leigh closed her eyes briefly. Sometimes it
seemed she'd prayed about nothing else in months.

"I will. I have." She opened her eyes and smiled

at her sister. "Now I'd better get showered. I have a shift at the restaurant tonight."

Leigh took the narrow lane slowly as she came home from the restaurant. The island didn't boast streetlights, and even longtime residents sometimes had trouble spotting their destinations in the dark, screened as they were by the lush, invasive vegetation. Live oaks lined the road, their veils of Spanish moss dancing in the soft Southern breeze, soothing her frazzled nerves.

No doubt about it; that encounter with Sarah had touched her heart. *Too vulnerable for your own good.* That was what her supervisor had said at their last meeting, and the words still stung. Yes, Sarah had found her vulnerable spot.

As for Daniel, the confrontation with him had raised a dragon she thought she'd already slain. Her decision had been made, she reminded herself. Daniel Gregory, with his proud eyes and his charming smile, couldn't change that.

She pulled into the driveway, its layer of shells crunching under her tires. A strange vehicle sat next to Jamie's elderly Toyota. She stared at the dark-blue pickup for a moment, certainty pooling in her mind. Daniel Gregory had come. The man wouldn't take no for an answer.

For a brief, cowardly moment she considered pulling right back out of the driveway. Then she got out, closed the car door and started toward the deck. Polite but firm; that was the line she had to take. Surely this time she could convince him that she meant what she said.

She crossed the deck and swung open the kitchen

door on a homey scene. Josh, Jamie and Daniel sat around the scrubbed oak table, coffee mugs cradled in their hands. One of Jamie's carrot cakes, half-demolished, sat between them. The three of them looked up as she came through the door, and for an instant they seemed allied against her.

Ridiculous. But the suspicion lingered, giving an edge to her smile.

"This looks cozy." She let the screen door close behind her. "Mr. Gregory, I didn't expect to see you again so soon."

"'Daniel.'" He half rose, then sat down again, his chocolate eyes assessing her.

"Daniel just dropped by," Jamie said, the words a little rushed. The faintest flush tinged her cheeks. "Would you like some cake?"

"I ate at the restaurant."

Actually, she'd managed to choke down only half a greasy hamburger, but Jamie didn't need to know that. It was clear her big sister had been meddling again, and Leigh wasn't about to encourage her.

"At least have a cup of coffee with us," Jamie pressed, shooting a sideways glance at Daniel.

Her sister wasn't being very subtle. "No, thanks. It'll keep me awake, and I'm beat." She stifled a yawn. "In fact, I think I'll go to bed." If Jamie had invited Daniel Gregory here to change her mind, Jamie could entertain him herself.

"Leigh, don't. I..." Jamie sputtered, glancing at her husband for help, but Josh appeared to be considering sliding under the table. Poor Josh. His fair skin blushed too easily.

"Don't go." Daniel's quiet words dropped into the fray, sending out circles of silence around them.

He gave her a slow smile that packed enough heat to raise the room temperature. "I want to talk to you."

"If Jamie called you..." Leigh began, but the sentence faded away. This wasn't a sisterly squabble anymore. This was between her and Daniel.

"It doesn't matter. I was coming over anyway." That mesmerizing look would stop a rampaging gator.

"Please, Leigh." Jamie found her voice again. "I didn't mean to interfere, but if you'll just listen to Daniel..."

"She might if we gave her a chance." Josh took Jamie firmly by the arm, urging her from the chair, and sent an apologetic glance toward Leigh. "Why don't the two of you go out on the deck." He piloted Jamie toward the living room. "You can have a little privacy there."

Daniel waited until they were out of the room, then held the kitchen door for her. He lifted one dark eyebrow. "Please?"

Leigh knew when she'd been outmaneuvered. There was nothing for it now but to listen to what the man had to say. Then she could tell him no in the most sympathetic way possible. She nodded stiffly and walked past him onto the deck.

Daniel followed her, letting the screen door swing closed. It shut the two of them into the quiet dark together.

She half expected him to plunge into speech, but he didn't. He crossed the deck, leaned his elbows on the railing and looked out across the salt marsh that stretched beyond the house to the tidal creek.

"Beautiful, isn't it?"

Unwillingly, she joined him, trying to frame the words she'd use to tell him no.

The nearly full moon sent pale light streaming across the patchwork of water, sand and grass. Impossible to tell where the dividing line was between solid ground and liquid mud. Sounds reached them, a rustle, a splash, the cry of some night creature. Leigh shivered.

"Beautiful and dangerous," she murmured.

"Yes." He turned toward her, and the light from the kitchen window struck his face. It showed her one side—strong bones, stubborn jaw, well-shaped mouth—and left the other in shadow. "Look, I...there's something I want to say to you."

Leigh braced herself for the demand she knew was coming. She couldn't...couldn't...say yes.

"I'm sorry," he said. "And thank you."

She blinked. "What?" Where was the offer she'd steeled herself to turn down?

"Thank you," he said again. His smile flashed, setting her skin tingling. The man's smile should come with a warning label. "For finding Sarah today, for being so good with her when she must have been scared to death. Thank you, Leigh."

The quiet words seemed to resonate, to carry more meaning than they should.

"It was...I mean, anyone would have done the same."

His jaw tightened. "I wasn't there for her. You were."

Now the pain beneath the words slid into view, like a creature surfacing in the marsh, and she didn't know how to respond. She suspected he wasn't a man who let his private pain be seen easily.

"We can't always be there for the people we love." Her mind flashed uneasily to Tommy, to her own failure, then shied away. "No matter how much we want to."

"No matter how much." He repeated her words. The shadows of the salt marsh moved fitfully as a cloud crossed the moon. "I guess that's my only excuse for putting you on the spot this afternoon. Pushing you to help with Sarah in front of your niece and nephew. I shouldn't have done that."

She could smile at it now. "They were pretty tough to get away from. It's okay."

"Now I've done it again." He gestured toward the house, his expression rueful. "Involved your family. I didn't mean to."

"I'm sure you didn't. Jamie called you, didn't she?" A small flame of anger warmed the words.

"Don't blame her." His lips twitched slightly. "Elder sisters and brothers are what they are. Believe me, I know."

"You have one?"

"I was one. The eldest, I mean."

Something darkened in his eyes at that, and she sensed inquires about his family wouldn't be welcome.

"I was coming to see you. Her call didn't change anything."

She wanted to argue, to say that Jamie had no right butting into her affairs, but that would probably make her sound about ten years old.

When she didn't respond he turned back to the

rail, where he leaned on his elbows. She seemed to have little choice but to do the same.

For a few moments they stood in silence, looking out at the moonlit marsh. Maybe he was concentrating on the view. She was too aware of the lean strength of his arm brushing hers, of the warmth that radiated from him.

"So," he said finally, interrupting a chorus of frogs, "you like your job?"

The smell of grease from her clothes and hair made it impossible to say anything but the truth. "Not especially. But it's only temporary. So I have some money coming in while I look for something else."

She was digging herself into a hole. She waited for him to ask why she was looking for a job and wondered what she'd say when he did. But he didn't.

"Guess that's kind of where I am, too. Caught in a situation I don't like."

She glanced at him, but the strong lines of his face didn't give anything away. "You mean Sarah?"

He braced both hands against the rail. "I don't regret anything about having my daughter."

"No, I didn't mean..."

"It's this way." He turned toward her with sudden energy, as if he'd made a decision. "You know about the new bridge they're building?"

The abrupt change of subject left her floundering. "Bridge?"

"Bridge from Athena Island," he said, naming the vacation mecca from which ferries ran to tiny St. Joseph's. "They've talked about building one for years, but now it's really going to happen. When it does, I have to be ready for it."

"Ready?" She felt like a parrot.

"I own beachfront property," he said, a hint of impatience in his voice. "Right now I just have a lodge—rent a few rooms to fishermen, the occasional tourist."

"But when the bridge is built..." She was finally beginning to catch up.

"The bridge will bring tourists, and tourists want beachfront rooms. That's what I'm doing. Building an addition that will double the number of rooms I have."

Somehow that was the last thing she'd expected. She'd assumed, if she'd thought about it at all, that Daniel was probably a fisherman, like Josh. He had a rugged look she associated with working outdoors.

"So," she said, trying to adjust her image of him, "you're going to be the Donald Trump of St. Joseph's Island."

"Nothing like that." He made an impatient gesture. "Just a small place. But enough to provide for Sarah. That's why I'm doing it. I have to provide for Sarah, and that takes money."

She remembered his words on the beach. "You want the money to send Sarah to school."

"I need the money." He leaned toward her, turning the full force of his personality on her. It was like standing in a hurricane. "I'm all Sarah's got, and I will provide for her. That's why I need you."

She couldn't turn away from the passion in his voice. "I..."

"I'm doing most of the work myself." He swept

on, not giving her a chance to respond. "Only way I can afford to do it. That means I work all day, every day. I have to have someone I trust to take care of Sarah."

"What makes you think you can trust me? You don't even know me!" No, it wasn't a hurricane she felt; it was an undertow. And it was pulling her under no matter how she struggled.

"I saw you with Sarah."

He stopped, as if that were all he needed to say. This strong, self-reliant, proud man stood looking at her with...not a demand. She could have handled a demand. A plea. He wanted—needed—her help, and he wasn't a person who asked for help easily. The pressure that had been building from the moment she walked into the kitchen broke over her.

She had to answer him, had to say something. Despairing, she knew what it was.

"I'll help." She held up her hand before he could say anything. "I'll help out, but only for a few days. Just until you can find someone reliable." What was she letting herself in for? "I mean it...just a few days, no longer."

Daniel clasped both her hands in his, and his warmth set her skin sizzling.

"You won't regret it, Leigh. I promise."

She already regretted it, but there was no point in telling him that. "I'll be there first thing in the morning. Josh can tell me how to find you."

"Right." His fingers tightened around hers, then he released her. "I'll see you tomorrow, then."

He turned away quickly, as if afraid to press his luck. "In the morning, then."

In a moment he was in his truck and backing out

the drive, leaving Leigh wondering just what kind of idiot she was.

You were going to tell him no, she reminded herself. *You weren't going to get involved.* A moment of panic swept over her. How was she going to bear it? To get to know Sarah, to be teaching again, even for a few days—it would hurt so much to give it up.

Just a few days. Daniel couldn't talk her into doing more, though he'd proved to be a master at getting what he wanted. He'd disarmed her with his apology, drawn her into his dreams for Sarah, put her in a position from which she couldn't say no.

He was an impossible man to say no to. He was the last man in the world she had any right being attracted to. That had to stop.

A few days, that was all. A breeze whispered over the marsh, bending the grasses, lifting the hair on her arms. She shivered. If Daniel thought she'd change her mind, he'd underestimated her. Daniel and Sarah were going to be a minor detour in the course she'd laid out for herself; that was all.

Chapter Three

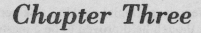

Leigh stopped at the end of the path the next morning, staring at the scene in front of her. Trumpet-shaped white and lavender flowers lifted their heads from fringes of beach grass. The sun gilded blue-gray water, and the beach stretched empty except for the occasional laughing gull. The receding tide left wet sand in a smooth layer of light toast.

The skeleton of Daniel's building rose in a sea of beach grass and wild roses—two stories of bare timbers, awkward and raw looking, out of place in this little piece of Eden.

Sarah played contentedly on a blanket spread in the shadow of a pile of lumber next to the construction. She wrapped a baby doll carefully in a scrap of pink blanket, then tucked it into a doll cradle, crooning something Leigh couldn't make out.

Leigh's heart clenched. *Only a few days,* she reminded herself. This would last only a few days. She couldn't become attached to Sarah.

Why was Sarah by herself? A movement caught her eye, and she realized several things at the same moment. Daniel worked, alone, on the second-story skeleton, and he watched Sarah as he did so. And, right now, he also watched her.

He stood, the movement taking him from shadow to sunlight, and her breath caught in her throat. He perched on what looked like an impossibly thin beam, balancing as effortlessly as a cougar on a tree limb. He was shirtless, and the slant of sunlight gilded skin and muscle as it did the ocean, making his flesh glow. Suddenly embarrassed to be caught staring, she raised her arm and waved.

Daniel nodded, put down his hammer and strode the length of the beam as easily as a gull skimming the water. He reached the end and swung himself down, sleek muscles moving under tanned skin.

She went toward him, sternly telling her breathing to get under control.

"I hope I'm not late."

He shrugged.

"I have to start early." His gesture took in the expanse of half-finished building. "Lots to do."

"You're doing it yourself?"

"One of the local contractors helps out when I need it."

She'd already figured out that money was in short supply. So there was no crew of carpenters, just Daniel Gregory working alone on his dream.

"Sarah's been fine down here, but you can take her to the house if you want."

"Maybe we'll stay here for a while. She might feel more comfortable near you at first."

He nodded. "You need anything just ask Joe. He knows everything."

Daniel's gaze strayed back to his construction, as if pulling his attention from it was a hardship. As if a flesh-and-blood woman couldn't compete with timber and nails. She squashed a wave of what might have been annoyance. She didn't want Daniel to be interested in her. The next few days would be difficult enough without that complication.

"Sarah and I will be all right. You go back to work and don't worry about her."

He turned away, then turned back again with that rare smile lightening his serious, contained face. "I'm glad you came, Leigh."

This was the moment to remind him that she'd agreed to watch Sarah only until he found someone else. Instead, she discovered that she was returning his smile, her gaze caught and held by his until he swung away from her.

She'd been right. That smile of his really *should* come with a warning label. Maybe its effect was intensified by its rarity.

She crossed the warm sand and dropped to her knees on the blanket next to Sarah.

"Hi, Sarah." She signed as she spoke. "I'm Leigh. Remember me?"

Sarah's dark eyes, so like her father's, surveyed Leigh solemnly for a moment. Finally a smile touched the corner of her mouth, and she nodded.

"That's a nice baby." Leigh patted the pink wrapped bundle. "Does she have a name?"

Sarah's mouth compressed in a firm line. She snatched the doll from the cradle, then carefully rewrapped it, fingers smoothing the blanket with care. Finally she replaced it in the cradle, crooning something unintelligible.

The message was clear. *Don't touch.* Without Meggie's ebullient presence, Sarah was going to be a tough nut to crack.

A half hour later, Leigh had revised her opinion. Not just tough. Nearly impossible. She sat back on her heels, exasperated, as Sarah repeated the routine with the baby doll for perhaps the tenth time. Leigh's mind seethed with questions, and she wanted to snatch Daniel from his ladder and pepper him with them.

How much residual hearing did Sarah actually have? Had she been to school? If not, who'd been teaching her? And what on earth did this routine with the doll and cradle mean?

You don't need to know that. You don't have the right to answers. This is only temporary, remember? That's what you want.

Well, temporary or not, she had to do her best. She clasped Sarah's hand before the business with the doll could begin again.

"Come on, Sarah. Let's go for a walk."

Sarah drew back, hanging heavily on Leigh's hand, looking at the doll.

"Daddy will watch the baby, okay? Daddy won't let her get hurt."

That seemed to do the trick. With a backward, reluctant look at the cradle, Sarah got to her feet. She let Leigh lead her away from the blanket.

They walked along the upper reaches of the sand, but when Leigh tried to take her down to the smooth, shimmering expanse left by the outgoing tide, Sarah balked.

"No!"

That word she verbalized well enough. Leigh suppressed a smile. Most children did if they talked at all.

"Why not?" Leigh persisted. "Meggie loves to play in the water. Don't you?"

Sarah stared at the ocean for a moment, lower lip extended. Then her hands moved. "Cold," she signed. "Too cold."

Fair enough. The water, warmed by southern ocean currents, seemed comfortable to Leigh, but maybe Sarah did find it cold.

The ebbing tide had left a legacy, though...an oblong, sandy tidal pool, its water warmed by the sun until it was probably the temperature of bathwater.

"Look at this." She led the reluctant child to the pool. "Look—a Sarah-sized pool." She knelt, then scooped a handful of water and let it trickle through her fingers. "Warm."

Sarah clasped her hands firmly, shaking her head. No one, it was clear, would convince her to put her hands in.

Leigh kicked off her sandals, sat down and dipped her toes in the warm pool. She'd always found that the best way to work with deaf children was to bombard their senses with experiences and words. She'd never taught on a beach before, but the principle had to be the same.

"Come on, Sarah," she coaxed. "Try it. It feels good."

It took fifteen minutes by Leigh's watch—fifteen

minutes of coaxing, teasing and patience—before Sarah pulled off her sandals and stuck a wary toe in the water. And then it took all of about fifteen seconds for her to be romping across the pool just as Meggie would, splashing the water so that both her shorts and Leigh's were soaked.

Grinning with a mix of pleasure and triumph, Leigh trickled water on Sarah's bare arm. It gained her a delighted giggle, the first she'd heard.

A shadow fell across them, shutting off the sun. "What on earth are you doing?" Daniel demanded.

As soon as the words were out of his mouth, Daniel realized how harsh they'd sounded. He couldn't help it. For a split second, before his brain told him Sarah was safe, he'd panicked at the sight of her in the water. He took a breath. She was okay.

Leigh stood up to her knees in the pool, her shorts thoroughly splashed, her expression wary. Sunlight glinted from droplets of salt water on her bare golden arms. Her eyebrows lifted. "Is something wrong?"

He wasn't going to get what he wanted by biting off her head. He made a conscious effort to soften his tone.

"Sarah hasn't gone anywhere near the water since she's been here. I think that's best."

Leigh glanced from him to Sarah, who was bent over, hands on knees, looking at something in the water. "Let me get this straight. You want her to be afraid?"

"Of course I don't want her to be afraid!" For

a moment he wished he were still dealing with a teenage baby-sitter. She might be careless, but at least she didn't argue with him. "But the surf is dangerous, and Sarah's not used to it. Besides, she's…"

"She's deaf," Leigh said quietly.

Those sea-green eyes of hers bored right into his soul.

"She's also a bright five-year-old who should be treated like one."

He held on to his temper with an effort. "And I'm not treating her right?"

"Well…"

It was so easy to read her expression that the edge of his anger dissolved into amusement. That was exactly what she thought, but she was too polite to say so.

"All right." He drove a hand through his hair. "You tell me. How do I keep her safe when she can't hear a warning?"

"That's one of the reasons she's wearing a hearing aid. So she can make the most of the hearing she has. She can hear things like the beep of a car horn, the screech of brakes, a train whistle. She wouldn't have an aid unless she has enough hearing for it to make a difference."

He jerked his head toward the surf. "No car horns out there."

"No, but she still has to learn." She smiled suddenly, sunlight on water. "Jamie and I grew up in the country. I can still remember our mother, every time she took us for a walk in the woods, going over her rules. 'Never put your hands or feet where your eyes can't see.'"

He must have looked blank. The smile became a grin.

"Because of snakes," she said. "Mom was deathly afraid of them, but she wouldn't let that keep us from enjoying the woods. If Sarah's going to live near the water, she has to learn safety precautions, just as a child in the Midwest learns what to do in case of a tornado."

"But..." His argument disappeared at the sight of Sarah. She wasn't romping across the pool now. She'd crawled out of the water, and she lifted her arms to him, her face clouding with tears.

He bent to pick her up, his throat tightening. "Honey, it's all right. What's wrong?"

"She knew we were arguing." Leigh's lips tightened. "Kids don't need to hear to know that. She knew you didn't like her being in the water."

He patted Sarah's back, trying to hold on to his conviction that he was right about this. But he couldn't.

"Okay." He said it reluctantly. "You win. We'll work out some way of teaching her what's safe to do on the beach."

She smiled, as if she'd known all along he'd agree. "Let's get her back in the water again, then."

"Joe will have lunch ready. We'd better go up. We can talk about it while we eat."

Leigh's mouth set. "We can't walk away now."

"Why not?" He tried to keep the exasperation from his tone. If she wasn't the most stubborn woman in the world, she came close.

"Never end a session on a negative note. Right

now, Sarah thinks the water is something to fear. She has to go back in again before we quit."

For a moment he just stared at her. "You must have been quite a teacher."

Something flickered in her eyes at that. Pain, maybe. He wondered again what was behind this determination of hers to leave teaching. He'd find out eventually, but now wasn't the time. He sat down on the sand, plopped Sarah down next to him and began unlacing his work boots.

"What are you doing?" Apprehension colored her question, and he grinned.

"Coming in the water." He pulled off boots and socks, then stood in the warm, shallow pool, letting the water lap his jeans to the knees. He held out his hand to Sarah. "Come on, sugar. Let's splash Leigh, okay?"

Sarah hesitated, then scooted forward a little.

He coaxed his daughter back into the water, then watched as she ran to Leigh. Sarah's solemn face crinkled into a smile he hadn't seen often enough, and his breath caught.

He could give up on Leigh. Find some nice, grandmotherly type who wouldn't do anything but sit on the porch and keep Sarah safe. But seeing Leigh with his daughter, he knew that wasn't enough, not anymore. Somehow, he had to see that Leigh stayed with Sarah for the summer.

As for his totally unsuitable urge to run his hand along her sun-kissed cheek, well, he'd just deal with it. One thing he'd learned the hard way—he'd never give his heart to a woman again.

"More rice, ma'am?" Joe held the pottery bowl of rice and shrimp out to Leigh across the round kitchen table. She'd already suggested twice that he call her "Leigh," but apparently it was going to be "ma'am" for a while.

"No, thanks. It was delicious." She glanced at Sarah, who was stirring her remaining rice around on her plate. "Good, wasn't it, Sarah?"

Leigh'd been signing throughout the meal, trying to draw Sarah into the conversation, but it had been futile. Daniel seemed uncomfortable with signing, and he used it haltingly only when he talked directly to Sarah.

She wasn't going to be here long enough to change the way they interacted, she reminded herself.

You have to try, the voice of her conscience prompted. *You have to try.*

Daniel's chair scraped. "Better get back to work."

He started for the door; she got up, too, and followed him to the porch, which wrapped around the old house like a blanket.

"Daniel, may I have a word before you go?"

He glanced at the path to the construction, then seemed to force his gaze back to her. "What is it?"

Maybe this wasn't a good time to broach the subject. He was impatient to get back to his precious hotel.

Coward, her conscience chided.

"It's about signing." She took a deep breath. He'd probably tell her it was none of her business, but she had to try. "I notice you don't sign very much."

His frown told her this wouldn't go well. "I'm no expert, if that's what you mean."

"Well, neither is Sarah, but she depends on it. When the people around a deaf child don't sign constantly, the child is left out of so much." She sounded as though she was giving a lecture, and his frown had deepened. "I don't mean to criticize. I just think if you made an effort to sign more…"

He swung away, and for an instant she thought he was going to walk off without even answering her. Then he turned back, his face set.

"You want to know why I don't sign very well I'll tell you. My wife took Sarah and left when my daughter was a year old, went clear up to Baltimore to live with her folks. Since then I've seen my daughter twice a month, for visits that were too short. Sure, I took lessons, but I guess that just wasn't enough to make me a pro at signing."

Then he did walk away.

Leigh leaned against the porch railing, wishing she could erase the last few minutes. She should have guessed that something like that had been wrong, but she'd been so preoccupied with her own problems that she hadn't thought it through.

Jamie probably knew some of this, but she hadn't said anything. Not that Leigh had given her much chance. She'd been too busy resenting Jamie's interference.

She bit her lip, looking down the path Daniel had taken. Should she go after him, apologize? Maybe that would make matters worse. Maybe she'd better just concentrate on Sarah for the time that was left. Because after the mess she'd made of that conversation, it was very unlikely that he'd be pressuring her to stay.

She turned and went back into the dining room. Joe poured another cup of coffee, his dark eyes wary and shuttered when he glanced toward her. He'd heard, of course. He couldn't have helped it.

"I think it's time Sarah showed me her room." She held her hand out to Sarah. "Unless we can help you with the dishes."

"No, ma'am. I don't need help."

And if he did need help, he wouldn't want it from her; that was clear. Well, naturally he would be on Daniel's side. But why did they have to choose sides? They all wanted what was best for Sarah.

It was almost time to leave, and what had she accomplished in her day? Leigh straightened the covers on Sarah's bed and glanced around the room.

Someone had made an effort to create a room a little girl would like. The flowered wallpaper and white woodwork suited the white wicker furniture. The well-used child's table and chairs looked like an afterthought, brought from someone's attic.

The baby doll and cradle were no longer in the room. Sarah had carried them downstairs with her a few minutes ago when she went down for milk and cookies with Joe.

Leigh fluffed up the pillow, then turned to the table where she'd been trying to get Sarah to paint. One picture—that was all Sarah had done before she'd gone back to the baby doll. Leigh smiled, picking up the picture. Only one, but it was charming.

Daniel, recognizable by the dark hair and blue jeans, stood on the second story of the construction. He held a hammer. Above him, the blue sky was decorated with fat seagulls, their white wings spread wide.

"Still working?"

She turned at the voice. Daniel leaned against the door frame, looking at her with a half smile. Some thread of tension eased inside her. At least he wasn't still angry.

"Just cleaning up." She held out the picture. "Look at this."

He took the paper, glanced at it, then looked at her, eyes startled. "Sarah did this?"

She smiled. "All by herself. I asked her to paint a picture of her family, and that's what she came up with. Great, isn't it?"

"I've never seen her paint. Or draw." He touched the figure holding the hammer. "I didn't even know we had paints."

"You didn't." Sarah's belongings consisted primarily of dolls, stuffed animals and toys suitable for a younger child. "I brought them."

"I guess I should have thought of that." He looked around the pink-and-white room. "Sarah's aunt bought most of this stuff for her. I wasn't sure what she'd like."

She probably shouldn't ask, but the question spilled out of her mouth anyway. "What about the doll and cradle?"

His expression grew wary. "What about it?"

"Did you buy it for her?"

"No." His mouth tightened. "Her aunt Judith did, I think. Anyhow, Judith said it was important to Sarah." His expression clearly said he didn't intend to pursue the subject. "You liked your day with Sarah." It was a statement, not a question.

"Yes." She took the picture back from him and fastened it to the closet door, where Sarah could admire her work. "Of course I did."

"Better than burgers and fried sweet potatoes?"

He was pressing her, and the only possible response was a light one. "I like fried sweet potatoes. Don't you?"

He took a step closer. "To eat, not to serve." He made an impatient gesture, as if sweeping away the burgers and sweet potatoes. "Sarah needs you. I want you to stay."

She'd already given him every reason but the real one. "I...please don't ask me again, Daniel. I just can't."

"Why not?" His dark eyes held hers, demanding an answer.

Anger flickered through her. This wasn't fair. "Look, I have my reasons. You don't have the right to push me for explanations."

"You pushed me."

She felt the heat flood her cheeks. She'd pressed him for answers, for explanations he'd been clearly reluctant to give. And now she expected him to coddle her tender feelings. Obviously he wasn't going to.

"I'm sorry for that."

He shook his head in a swift, determined motion. "You did it because you care about Sarah. Now I want answers for the same reason."

The mixture of pain and love in his dark eyes undid her. The moment when she could have walked away was gone. She knew both of them too well already. She turned from that gaze and moved to stare out the white-curtained window at sea and sky.

"I let you believe I quit teaching." It took an effort to keep her voice steady. "That's not quite true. I was fired."

"Why?"

His neutral tone surprised her. She'd expected...well, shock, at least.

She took a deep breath. "I taught at a private school...small classes, lots of time to give individual attention. There was one child, Tommy." Her heart hurt when she thought of Tommy, of how she'd failed him. "He was going through a bad time, his parents splitting up." Too late she remembered that Daniel's wife had left him.

"The kid was caught in the middle."

She nodded. "I tried to help. The father seemed more approachable, so I talked to him, looked for ways we could help Tommy deal with it. Tommy had been making such progress up to then, really coming out of his shell. I didn't want to see him slip back."

She rubbed her arms, cold in spite of the heat of the day. Daniel stood perfectly still behind her, and she didn't want to see his expression.

"Then it all blew up in my face. The mother found out I'd met with her husband. She accused me of interfering, of improper conduct—" She stopped, flushing at the memory of the horrendous scenes. "She threatened to sue me and the school."

"So they fired you."

She nodded. "It was the only way out for them. The publicity alone could have damaged the school. She finally agreed to drop the suit if they got rid of me. So they did."

"What does that have to do with Sarah?"

For a moment she froze, sure she hadn't heard him correctly. Then she swung toward him.

"Don't you understand? The lawsuit, the adults—that's not important. What's important is the child! I failed Tommy. My bad judgment, my stupid pride, thinking I had all the answers...and Tommy was the one who suffered for it."

"What happened to him?"

Leigh had to swallow her tears at the memory. "He retreated into himself. He stopped trying. And it was because I failed him."

She forced herself to look at Daniel. His strong face was a mask, giving away nothing. Then he turned. Walked away.

She took a ragged breath, trying to hold the guilt at bay. She'd finally convinced him she wasn't a fit person to care for his child. He wouldn't be bothering her about that anymore.

She heard his footsteps cross the hall, then he was coming back. He thrust something into her hands...a photograph in a heart-shaped frame.

"Look at that." His fingers were strong on hers. "That's Sarah a few days before she and her mother left."

She looked. Daniel, holding a chubby baby with

dark hair. Love shone from a face that was more open than she'd seen since she met him.

"You don't have a monopoly on failure, Leigh." His voice gentled. "Believe me, I know all about it."

He obviously felt the breakdown of his marriage was his fault. She didn't know how to respond to that, but he didn't seem to expect her to.

"The only question for me is whether you'll be good for Sarah. And I know the answer to that."

She blinked back treacherous tears. Daniel, knowing her past and still wanting her to stay, didn't remove the main obstacle, not for her.

If she stayed, if she spent the summer with Sarah, it would hurt so much to leave. But maybe, in a way, it would atone for failing Tommy. How could she stay? How could she not?

"I'll sweeten the pot." Daniel's lips curved in that undermining smile. "If you stay, I'll let you teach me signing."

"You'll..."

He put his hands on hers, sending warmth along her skin. "Show me. Show me how to sign, Will you stay?"

Stubborn. Determined to get his own way. Too quick to find her own weak spots. She could foresee one battle after another over his plans for Sarah. She should run as fast as she could in the other direction.

She showed him.

"Will you stay?" he asked, signing. "Will you teach me?"

That just might be the most dangerous thing of all, she thought. She signed the words. "I'll stay."

Chapter Four

Daniel let out a breath. He'd done it. He'd convinced Leigh to take care of Sarah for the summer. No matter what else happened, he'd begun to fulfill his promise to his daughter. She was going to get the best money could buy.

As for Leigh's past troubles... He found he didn't care what she'd done, as long as she was good for Sarah. He could go back to work with a clear conscience.

"That's settled, then. I'll see you in the morning." He turned toward the door, to be stopped by a hand on his arm.

"Settled?" He glanced at Leigh, saw her eyebrows arch at the question. "It's far from settled."

Was she backing out on him already? He swung toward her, and at his movement she snatched her hand away, as if she'd just touched sun-baked sand.

"If this is about the money, I'll pay whatever the going rate is. You tell me."

She looked offended. "It's not about money."

"What, then? You said…"

"I said I'd work with Sarah for the summer." Her green-as-glass eyes frowned at him. "If I'm going to do that, and do it right, there's a great deal more I need from you."

The clock was ticking. If he didn't get back to work soon, it would be time for Joe to leave. Daniel would have to quit work then to be with Sarah, whether he was finished or not.

"Is that really necessary now? I've got about two hours of work to finish today."

That deceptively soft mouth set in a firm line. "I'm not a baby-sitter, Daniel. If I'm going to work with Sarah, I have to see her medical records, information from her last school, anything that will help me understand her."

He shrugged, impatient. "I'll round up the stuff and give it to you tomorrow, okay?"

Daniel had taken a couple of steps toward the door, when he realized she was shaking her head again. A reluctant respect for her tenacity swept through him.

"What?"

"We have to sit down together and talk about this." Her tone sharpened. "Sometime soon. When you're not in such a hurry. We need to develop a learning plan for her together."

He resisted the urge to tell Leigh to handle it herself. She wouldn't; he knew that much about her already. "All right." He ran a hand through his hair, exasperated. "When do you want to get together? I need the daylight hours for working."

"What about tonight?"

Tonight he'd be dog-tired from working all day. But it looked as if that didn't matter.

"All right, tonight. It'll have to be here, though. Joe leaves at six, so I have to be with Sarah."

"Fine. I'll come over around eight, if that's not an imposition."

He had a feeling there might be just a little sarcasm in those words. "Look, I do want to meet with you." He gripped her arm to add reassurance to the words. "I just…"

Whatever he'd been about to say trailed off as her skin warmed beneath his fingers. A betraying flush rose in her cheeks. His eyes met hers…met and held.

He wanted to run his hand down her arm. Quickly, before he could give in to the urge, he stepped back. He couldn't do this.

Leigh cupped her hand over the place where his fingers had been. Her green eyes darkened with confusion.

He cleared his throat. "Tonight. I'll have all Sarah's records ready."

"Fine." She seemed to be having the same difficulty with her voice that he was with his. "I'll be here at eight."

She spun and hurried out of the room before he could say another word.

Daniel went slowly down the steps in her wake. He couldn't stand there thinking about the warmth of a woman's skin or speculating about the softness of her mouth. He had to get back to work.

But he wondered—he surely did wonder—just what he was letting himself in for. Leigh was…he shook his head. Someone like Leigh was out of his experience. When Ashley left, he'd convinced himself he was better off alone. Looked like he needed to remind himself of that a few more times.

Leigh pulled the car into Daniel's driveway that night and glanced at her watch. Eight o'clock. She was right on time. She took a deep breath. Too bad she wasn't ready to face Daniel Gregory again.

Those moments alone with Daniel in Sarah's room today—how had they happened? One minute she'd felt nothing beyond a certain mild irritation with him. The next minute he'd touched her, and irritation had been totally washed away by the pull between them, a pull so powerful it frightened her.

And he had felt it, too. She knew it. He'd drawn away from her, looking as if danger signals flashed in front of his eyes.

Well, she wasn't going to get that close again. She'd keep this on a strictly businesslike basis.

Leigh inspected herself as best she could in the rearview mirror. Given the fact that nobody on the island dressed up in the summer except for church, she'd done the best she could to look professional.

She smiled. Her former supervisor at the school in Philadelphia certainly wouldn't consider a denim skirt and cotton sweater dressed for success. But on the island it was practically formal wear.

Somehow she suspected it was what she said and felt rather than what she wore that would either keep this situation under control or let it spin into something else. It was bad enough that she'd let herself be drawn into working with Sarah. It would be far worse if she let herself feel anything for Daniel.

For an instant her hands tightened on the steering wheel, and then she closed her eyes in a brief prayer—for wisdom, for detachment, for God's will.

She opened her eyes. She was as ready as she'd ever be. She got out and started for the family side of the rambling old house. The other side, where the inn sign creaked in the breeze, was dark.

Daniel opened the door before she had a chance to knock.

"Leigh." He stood back, holding it wide. "Come in. I've been waiting for you."

Maybe she was imagining the warmth in his voice. She certainly wasn't imagining the fact that the professional chat she'd planned was going to be difficult when he looked so...appealing.

His dark hair was still slightly damp from his shower, and his skin glowed with vitality against the clear aqua of his cotton sweater. The wariness had vanished from his eyes, at least for the moment. He was as relaxed as she'd ever seen him. So why did that make her nervous?

She glanced into the living room. Soft light from the table lamps spilled onto a sofa that was piled with colorful cushions. File folders covered the coffee table.

"Joe left some coffee for us. Okay?"

"Sounds good." She visualized the two of them, side by side on that soft couch. "I can come into the kitchen..." A nice bright kitchen seemed somehow better for her peace of mind.

But he shook his head. "I'm all set up in the living room. Besides, I might not hear Sarah call from back there."

She couldn't argue with that. She wandered into the living room while he pushed through the swinging door that led to the kitchen.

He hadn't invited her to look through the files yet, so she resisted the urge to flip them open, though her fingers itched to do so. Instead she moved around the room, wondering at it.

The furniture was old enough to be battered and not old enough to be called antique. Someone had made an effort to make the room appealing, painting the walls a pale cream and disguising mismatched upholstered pieces with bright cushions. Daniel's handiwork? Or had his wife done that before she left?

She'd seen the photograph on the bookcase the moment she walked in the room. It drew her irresistibly. She picked up the heavy pewter frame.

The woman who stared back at her had been caught by the camera in the doorway of this room, hands out to the frame on either side. Dark auburn hair spilled in curls to beyond her shoulders, framing a porcelain, heart-shaped face. The woman's eyes were lit with some emotion...was it love? Her parted full lips seemed about to speak.

"That was my wife. Ashley."

Leigh winced at the sound of Daniel's voice. The last thing she'd wanted was to be caught prying. She set the frame back in place, as if it was terribly important that it be exactly as it had been.

Then she turned to Daniel. "She was very lovely."

Daniel concentrated on finding room for the coffee on the laden table. He didn't so much as glance toward the photograph.

Did he keep it out all the time, a reminder of the wife who'd left him? Perhaps it had just been out since Sarah had come, to help her remember her mother.

"Yes," he said after the silence had stretched on too long. "She was beautiful."

He said it as though it didn't give him much pleasure.

"When did she—" Leigh stopped, appalled at herself. She had no right to ask a personal question, not when she was trying so hard to keep this professional.

Daniel poured coffee into a cup and handed it to her, drawing her over to the couch. "Three months ago."

He bit off the words, and Leigh was sure he wouldn't say more. She certainly wouldn't ask him.

He poured his own coffee, sat down and frowned at nothing in particular. "She was killed in a car accident."

"I'm so sorry." Sorry for him, sorry for Sarah, sorry she'd brought it up.

"Ashley always wanted to be a singer." Daniel's voice flattened. He might have been talking about someone he'd never known. "When she left the island, she started taking singing jobs wherever she could find them. Every one was going to be her big break." His fingers tightened on the cup, and she realized the apparent detachment didn't exist. "She went head-on into a bridge abutment on her way back from a club job in Columbus."

Tell me how to deal with this, Lord. I'm in over my depth. She sat down next to him, as if the mere presence of another human being might help.

''That must have been terrible for Sarah. And for you.''

His mouth tightened, compressing into a thin, straight line. ''Most people don't see it that way. After all, we'd gone separate ways for four years.''

''She was still the mother of your child.'' And once, they'd promised to love each other forever. A person like Daniel couldn't just get over that, not easily. Maybe not ever.

She reached out, involuntarily, and then drew her hand back. She longed to touch him in a gesture of comfort, but the memory of what had happened the last time they touched stopped her. Comforting Daniel wouldn't be like holding Meggie when she'd fallen. Comforting Daniel could carry her into deep water far too quickly.

''Yes. She was Sarah's mother.''

His eyes darkened. For a moment she thought he'd say more, but then he reached for one of the file folders on the table.

''Here are the records you asked to see.''

He'd shut the door on confiding in her, and she wasn't surprised. She didn't think Daniel would easily let another person into the place where the real man dwelled, beyond the external facade of strength and competence. However much he might hurt, he wouldn't want someone else to see.

She flipped open the first file. Concentrate on Sarah—that was what she had to do. Daniel Gregory's pain was private. She had no right to pry.

For the next half hour nothing broke the silence but the rustle of pages, the soft clink of a cup against a saucer. Leigh read slowly, sometimes going back to look again. The medical records first, dating back to Sarah's first visits to the pediatrician.

She could read between the lines of those early records, could imagine the pain and denial that lay behind the stark words. She'd seen it too many times…the loving parents, delighted with their perfectly beautiful, perfectly healthy baby. The gradual realization that something wasn't right. The repeated visits to the doctor, the assurances that everything was fine, followed by the knowledge that it wasn't.

The tests, the specialists. The final pronouncement. Their beautiful baby would never be just like everyone else. Sarah had a serious hearing impairment.

But she wasn't profoundly deaf. Leigh shuffled through the reports until she found the most recent test results. Sarah did have some hearing, enough so that hearing aids could help her. That was encouraging. With the right teaching…

There didn't seem to have been much teaching. Leigh frowned, looking for school records. Sarah had been enrolled in a preschool program that had started in the fall. Her attendance had been erratic, and finally ceased entirely in March. March, probably when her mother died.

Leigh looked up to find Daniel's dark eyes fixed on her face. "I notice Sarah hasn't been to school much." She tried to keep that from sounding judgmental, but Daniel frowned.

"I pushed Ashley about whether Sarah should be in school, but she didn't think so. Or maybe it was her family who didn't think much of the idea. They kept telling me that Sarah did better at home, where she was safe. Her aunt Judith taught her.''

Careful, careful. Don't get him defensive. ''Does her aunt have training in working with children with hearing impairment?''

His jaw tightened. ''No. But she does care a great deal about Sarah. Isn't that important with a child this young?''

''Yes, of course.'' Did Daniel really believe Sarah's aunt had known best? Or was his pride hurt because other people had been making decisions about his daughter's care? ''But we find that children usually do well in a structured situation with a qualified teacher. The presence of other children helps, too.''

''Do you really teach a young child?'' He looked skeptical. ''Or is it just playing?''

The barriers were still there. Leigh had dealt with enough reluctant parents to know that.

''Children learn through playing.'' She smiled, willing him to listen, to understand. ''They learn through all kinds of things that aren't formal instruction. When I work with Sarah, I'll use as many of her senses as possible to involve her. Since she has some hearing, this will encourage her to verbalize. I hope you won't dismiss something as 'just playing' without asking me about it.''

A smile teased at his mouth in response. ''So if I find you splashing in a tidal pool, for instance, that's a lesson?''

''Absolutely.'' She relaxed, just a little. He did seem to understand. So maybe she ought to bring up the other thing that bothered her. ''It would help if I knew a little more about your plans for Sarah when school starts in the fall.''

''I've enrolled her in the Spring Valley School. Do you know it?''

Spring Valley was one of the oldest residential schools for deaf children in the country. ''I'm familiar with their program.''

Daniel's eyebrows lifted. ''That doesn't sound very enthusiastic. What's wrong with it? I was told it's the best of its kind.''

''It probably is.'' Leigh made an effort to tread lightly. ''If a residential program is right for Sarah, you couldn't find a better one.''

''That's it, then.'' He set his cup down with a final click. ''Sarah's going to have the best, no matter how much it costs.''

She couldn't hold back the question that filled her mind. ''Have you thought about keeping Sarah at home and sending her to a regular school with some extra help? She could—''

''No.'' His expression closed down again. ''Sarah couldn't get along in a regular school. I'm not going to put her in a situation where other kids make fun of her. It's out of the question.''

He didn't want to listen; that was clear.

''But with the amount of hearing she has—''

Leigh's words cut off at the sound from above them. A thump, followed by a cry. Daniel shot from the couch and across the room. Leigh hurried after him.

Sarah. Something had happened to Sarah.

Upstairs, Daniel bolted into the darkness of Sarah's room. Leigh stopped in the doorway, groping along the wall for the switch. After what seemed an eternity, she found it, pressed it, flooded the room with light.

Sarah sat on the floor next to her bed. Both hands were clenched; her eyes were screwed shut. One piercing cry after another came from her mouth. Daniel, his face anguished, tried to hold her, but she stiffened, lurching backward in his arms.

"Daniel..." Leigh went to them.

He shot her a look over Sarah's head, a look that seemed to say, *You see? She can't cope in a normal environment.*

She knelt beside them. "Night terrors," she said quietly. "My nephew has them sometimes. Jamie always takes him clear out of the bedroom, lets him wake up entirely. You can't soothe them back to sleep when they're that frightened."

Daniel didn't argue, didn't tell her she had no right giving him advice. He picked Sarah up, ignoring her screams, and carried her out of the room.

No, not ignoring, Leigh corrected, as she hurried after. She could see the pain he tried to hide behind that rigid expression. It hurt any parent to be unable to comfort a child. How much more it must hurt Daniel, struggling to be both father and mother to his child.

Daniel stopped at the bottom of the stairs, throwing a helpless look toward Leigh. Sarah's screams pierced the house. If there were any guests in the inn's rooms, they'd wonder what on earth was happening.

"The kitchen," Leigh said, without thinking about it. The kitchen always seemed the heart of any home. Maybe its normality would soothe Sarah.

The bright overhead light in the kitchen reflected

whitely from cabinets and appliances. "Come on, now, Sarah." Leigh kept her voice calm, normal. She pulled out a chair for Daniel and pushed him and the screaming child into it. "Everything's okay. Daddy's here. Leigh's here." She frowned at Daniel. "Talk to her."

"Why? She can't hear me." Daniel tried to pat Sarah, holding her closer as she struggled.

Probably not, without her hearing aid, but that didn't matter. Leigh put her hand on his chest for an instant, feeling the beat of his heart. "She'll feel it." She pulled her hand away. "Try it."

His look said he didn't buy it, but he'd try. "Come on, sugar, it's all right. It was just a bad dream." He stroked her back, his hand large against Sarah's tiny body. "Come on, little girl, you don't need to cry anymore."

The screams lessened, just a fraction. With a startled look at Leigh, Daniel held his daughter closer against his chest. He murmured one soothing sentence after another, over and over.

It seemed to take forever. Gradually Sarah's screams slowed, changed into sobs, then sniffles. Finally her eyes opened, and she looked from Daniel to Leigh.

"You're okay," Leigh signed, taking a breath for what seemed the first time since she'd heard that scream. "You're awake now, aren't you?"

Sarah nodded, sniffling, an involuntary sob escaping. Daniel stroked her back.

"The bulb must have burned out in the lamp." Daniel's eyes were dark with guilt. "She always has to have a light on. I should have checked it."

It sounded as if Daniel needed soothing, too.

"Why don't I make us some hot chocolate. If you have any, that is."

Daniel jerked a nod toward the bottom cabinet. "There's a tin in there. But shouldn't we get her back to bed?"

"I'd let her calm down a bit more first." Leigh rummaged for a saucepan. "That's what Jamie always does, anyway, and it appears to work." She smiled. "My sister's a pro when it comes to dealing with night terrors."

"Your nephew really does..." He looked down at Sarah. "I thought it was just Sarah. She's done it three or four times since she came. I didn't know what was wrong."

She could sense his guilt at not knowing. "The first time I heard Mark scream I thought we were being attacked by monsters. Jamie never turned a hair." Leigh put the saucepan on the big old-fashioned range, then touched Sarah and smiled. "You like hot chocolate? It's Meggie's favorite."

Sarah nodded vigorously, then leaned back against her father's chest. She hiccuped a time or two, but the unreasoning fear had disappeared entirely. Her eyes, bright with interest, watched Leigh.

Leigh went on talking, almost at random, about Mark's night terrors, about how Jamie insisted Leigh used to do that, but Leigh didn't remember a thing about it. She suspected Daniel needed the soothing assurance just as much as Sarah had. The smell of chocolate slowly filled the kitchen with its own comfort.

When the cocoa steamed, Leigh poured it into thick china mugs and put them on the table. She sat down across from Daniel and Sarah and pantomimed blowing on the hot liquid. Sarah followed her example, her little face solemn and intent.

Daniel's eyes met Leigh's. "Thank you." His smile seemed to take an effort. "You really are something."

Leigh shrugged, her cheeks warming at the unexpected praise. "Just a little personal experience."

"Experience I should have had with my own daughter." The depth of bitterness in his voice cut deep. "I guess I'm not very well prepared for being a single parent."

"You can't blame yourself for that." Or maybe he could. She didn't know—probably would never know—what had led to his estrangement from his wife, but he appeared to be doing his best for Sarah. "Anyway, blaming doesn't get you anywhere. Whatever you need to know, you can learn."

"Sarah shouldn't have to wait while I learn how to be a better father." His tanned hand, dark against the white china, steadied the cup while Sarah drank.

Leigh smiled. "I don't think Sarah feels that way. She's perfectly happy with the father she has."

For a moment she thought he'd argue, but he just shook his head and settled his arm more comfortably around his daughter.

Sipping the warm, sweet chocolate, Leigh watched them. Her heart clenched when Daniel stroked his daughter's hair. They were so right together, and Daniel didn't even realize it. He was what Sarah needed more than anything right now. The reassurance of his presence, the sense of his love.

She thought again of his determination to send

Sarah off to a residential school. Convinced it was best for her, he'd work himself half to death trying to provide it. He was so convinced that he wouldn't even consider any other possibility.

Maybe that was her job. Maybe that was really God's hand at work in her encounter with Sarah, in Daniel's insistence that she teach her.

If she could help Sarah learn to function in a regular school, so that she could live here with her father... The idea felt like the answer to all her questions.

She looked at Daniel, head bent as he murmured something to Sarah, who looked up at him with a world of trust and love in her face.

If she could do that for Daniel and Sarah by the time she left the island, maybe her own guilt would be soothed, as well.

Chapter Five

"**V**ery nice." Leigh stood behind Sarah, looking into the mirror over the dresser as she brushed Sarah's hair. By the time she arrived Sarah had had her breakfast, but she was only half-dressed. Leigh gave one more stroke to the child's thick dark hair, then put down the brush.

"Pretty girl," she signed, pointing to Sarah's reflection in the mirror. She made the circle of her face, followed by the tug on an imaginary bonnet string. "Pretty girl."

Sarah swung around, face contorted, and snatched Leigh's hand away. "No!" she said. She batted at Leigh's hand. "No!" She ran across the room and crawled back onto her bed.

Leigh just stood there for a stunned moment. What had brought that on? *Dear Lord, show me what to do.*

Someone or something had convinced this child she wasn't pretty. Leigh's mind flashed to the beautiful woman in the photograph in Daniel's living room. Her mother? The aunt who seemed to have done much of the raising of her? Who could have done that to a child?

Leigh crossed to the bed, where she bent to pick up Sarah's socks and shoes. *Keep it light,* she cautioned herself.

"*I* think you're pretty," she said. She smiled. "And I think I am, too. Two pretty girls. Now, let's get shoes on so we can play."

Sarah stared at her, dark eyes unreadable. Then she sat up and extended her foot toward Leigh.

"You can do it yourself," Leigh said cheerfully, holding the sock out to Sarah. "I know you can."

Sarah didn't seem to think so. She leaned back on the flowered quilt, as floppy as a rag doll. Obviously no one had been encouraging her to do anything for herself.

Leigh put the sock in Sarah's hand. "I'm going to make something with clay. Put your socks and shoes on, and you can, too."

Not waiting to see what Sarah did, Leigh turned away and sat down at the small table where she'd set out the clay, along with doll-sized dishes and a rolling pin. She busied herself rolling out a piece of clay, carefully not looking at Sarah. Maybe this wasn't exactly orthodox teaching, but she was convinced that Sarah could do far more than anyone seemed to expect.

She found her mind drifting back to the woman who'd left Daniel. It was hard to understand, harder still to understand why, after taking Sarah away, she'd apparently been content to leave much of her care to others. Hadn't she realized...

Her thoughts were interrupted by a small tug on

her sleeve. She turned. One sock was folded down and one wasn't, but they were both on. And Sarah had pulled on the sneakers, as well.

''Good job, Sarah!'' Leigh's hands flew with her enthusiasm. She'd known Sarah could do it. ''Good job!''

The tiniest of smiles peeked out. Leigh thought the little girl was going to verbalize something, but then she turned to the clay. She frowned and poked it with the tip of one small finger.

''It's okay,'' Leigh assured her. She'd noticed Sarah's reluctance to get her hands dirty. ''The clay won't stick to your hands. See?'' She held out her own hands. ''Try it.''

Sarah sent an uncertain glance toward the baby doll in its cradle. Leigh held her breath, seeing the longing in Sarah's eyes. Then Sarah slid onto the chair and picked up the rolling pin.

All right. Leigh still didn't know what the business with the doll and the cradle meant, but her instincts told her that the more she could involve Sarah with other things, the better. Working with clay, painting, maybe a walk on the beach later…

And other children. That was a key to unlocking the silent mystery that was Sarah; she was sure of it. Other children wouldn't let her withdraw. They'd pull her out, one way or another.

Mark and Meggie would be a start. She'd already spoken to Jamie about it, and Jamie agreed. The tricky thing would probably be getting Daniel to cooperate. As far as she could tell, he'd shielded his daughter from contact with anyone outside since she'd come to live with him.

Just as he seemed to shield himself, too. Cautious

questioning of Jamie had produced mixed results. Jamie said people on the island thought well of Daniel, considered him a hard worker and a good man, but also found him a bit of a loner.

As for women...Jamie had answered the question Leigh hadn't asked. Plenty of them had been interested after Ashley left, but Daniel politely discouraged any attempts to get him involved in a social life. At first he immersed himself in work. Then he had his daughter and his hotel. He didn't have time for anything else.

Leigh rolled the clay into a pretend pie, then cut it in slices. Her face intent, Sarah followed suit.

If Jamie had made any guesses about her interest in Daniel, she hadn't said anything, thank goodness. Leigh was concerned only because of how it affected Sarah, she told herself. That was all.

The day slid away. Sarah bounced back and forth between involvement in Leigh's activities and withdrawing to the safety of the doll and the cradle.

Leigh found she had to give herself a pep talk the fifth or sixth time that happened. She was making progress. She couldn't expect the child to give up established patterns in a day or two. It would happen.

"Come on, Sarah." She held out her hand. "Let's go down to the kitchen and see Joe. I have an idea."

Joe turned from the sink when they invaded his space. He gave Leigh a wary glance. "You ladies ready for a snack?"

"Not just yet." Leigh crossed her fingers. "I wonder if you'd let us use your kitchen for a while. Sarah and I want to make muffins."

He stared at her, his dark face impassive. Then he pulled something from a drawer and handed it to her. An apron.

Sarah soon sat at the kitchen table, enveloped in a vast white apron. Leigh, similarly attired, sat across from her.

"We're going to make muffins for supper, okay?"

Sarah looked a little doubtful.

"We can bake," Leigh said, signing. She turned to Joe, determined to get a positive response from him at least once. "We can bake. Right, Joe?"

He watched her sign, but his hands didn't move. Finally he nodded.

Okay, so Joe wasn't going to be an immediate convert. She'd get him in the end. Leigh pushed the flour and the measuring cup closer to Sarah. "You get the flour, Sarah. One cup."

Ten minutes later a fair amount of the flour had landed on the floor, but Sarah, on her knees, leaned eagerly over the table.

"Where's the egg?" Leigh asked, hiding it behind the flour. "Where is it, Sarah?"

Sarah smiled and pointed.

"There it is. Oops, it's gone again." Leigh slid it into her apron pocket.

"There!" Sarah shouted.

"Good talking, Sarah." Leigh palmed the egg, then rediscovered it in Sarah's apron.

Sarah laughed out loud.

The laughter clutched at Leigh's heart. That was a first. Please God, there'd be many firsts yet to come with this precious child.

"Okay." She held up the egg. "You say 'egg' and then we'll put it in. Okay?"

She held her breath. So far *no* and *there* were the only words she'd heard Sarah verbalize.

Sarah frowned at the paper muffin cups. She reached for the egg. "Egg," she said firmly, and snatched it.

"All right!" Leigh helped her crack it. "Good talking, Sarah. Good talking!"

Daniel's breath caught in his throat. He'd stood in the doorway for several minutes, not noticed by the three busy people in the kitchen. And what a reward he'd gotten for his patience. Sarah smiling. Sarah talking.

Just two words, he reminded himself. Still, it was a start. He'd known from the first moment he'd seen Leigh that she would be good for Sarah.

His gaze lingered on Leigh's slim form, which was swathed in a white apron that had to be one of Joe's. There was a dusting of flour on her chin, and another on the seat of her shorts, where she'd undoubtedly wiped off her hand.

Laughing, Leigh and Sarah dropped some sort of batter into a tray of paper cups, getting a fair amount of it on the table in the process. Nobody seemed to mind. Even Joe was laughing, leaning over to watch.

Daniel swallowed hard. It was a scene he might once have hoped to walk in on with Ashley and Sarah. A scene that had never existed, he reminded himself. Ashley hadn't been the domestic sort. He couldn't imagine her baking anything, and certainly not cheerfully creating a mess just to earn a word and a laugh from Sarah.

Leigh seemed so right somehow in his house, with his daughter. They might have been a family.

He yanked his mind away from that treacherous thought. Sarah was all the family he had, and all he wanted. He'd learned the hard way not to trust his heart to anyone else. Leigh was only there to teach Sarah, not to create daydreams for him that would never come true.

"Hey." He crossed to Sarah and bent to drop a kiss on her head. "What are you doing?" Mindful of Leigh's eyes on him, he signed the question.

Sarah dipped a spoon into the batter, then held it out to him. His heart swelled at the anxious look in her eyes.

He licked the spoon, then rubbed his stomach. "Delicious." He dropped another kiss on her nose. "Almost as delicious as my Sarah."

He looked up and caught another apprehensive glance, this time from Leigh. "We were baking," she explained unnecessarily.

Did she think he was upset at this unscholarly approach to teaching Sarah? "I can see that," he said. "Are we going to eat whatever this is?"

"Muffins," she said quickly. "You bet. You're going to have them for supper, and you're going to rave about them. And about the baker."

He eyed the voluminous apron she wore. "I won't find that hard at all."

"Not me." Her cheeks seemed to warm under his gaze. "Sarah. Sarah had a good day. She made things with clay and she painted and she baked."

And she smiled more than she has since she came

to live with me, he added silently. "That's great."
He touched his daughter's soft cheek. "Do these go
in the oven now?"

"For sure." Joe lifted the pan and slid it into the
huge oven he didn't let anyone else use. "Supper
be on in twenty minutes."

Daniel glanced toward the clock. "You've stayed
past your time." He turned to Leigh, watching as
she unwrapped herself from the apron. "I owe you
overtime."

"We were having fun." She bent over Sarah,
helping her with her apron. "Nobody owes me anything for that."

"But we agreed on your hours." And he didn't
accept charity, not from anyone. Bitter memories
from his childhood threatened to surface, and he
forced them back into the cellar of his mind. "It's
only fair."

Leigh started to reach for the bowl, but he
clasped her hands. Her gaze darted up to his, wide-
eyed, a little startled maybe.

"You don't owe me anything," she said firmly.
"Now, I'd better get this mess cleaned up, or Joe
won't let us in his kitchen again."

Joe slid the bowl efficiently out from under their
hands, then grabbed the other utensils in one sweep.
"I'll take care of this, ma—Leigh." He smiled.
"You and Sarah can take over my kitchen any-
time."

"Well." Leigh straightened, her cheeks pink.

Daniel realized he still held her hands. He let go
reluctantly.

"I guess I'll be on my way, then." She bent

closer to Sarah. "Goodbye, Sarah. I'll see you in the morning."

Sarah nodded, then gave her a sweet, grave smile. She waved goodbye.

Leigh waved back and turned to the door. And Daniel realized he didn't want her to go. Not until he'd thanked her properly, at any rate.

"I'll walk you to your car."

He followed her out. Their feet made little noise on the carpet of pine needles as they walked under the trees. Daniel took a breath of pine-scented air, tilting his head back. Every needle of the loblolly pines seemed etched against the sky.

Leigh followed his glance. "It's beautiful," she said quietly. Her gaze moved to his face. "You love this place, don't you?"

"Sea islands have been home all my life." Bittersweet memories touched him. "I can't imagine living in a place where you can't see the water."

That had been part of what went wrong with Ashley. She'd never understood his feelings about the place. She'd always been looking for bright lights, excitement.

"I'm beginning to understand that about islanders," Leigh said.

He shrugged. "It's probably pretty dull for someone like you."

"Dull?" She sent him a startled look. "I don't find it dull at all." She smiled. "Especially not since I met Sarah."

They stopped at her car, and he put his hand against the driver's side door. "I want to thank you again for what you're doing with Sarah."

"It's my job, remember? I love—" She stopped

abruptly, as if remembering it was a job she was determined to leave behind.

"You love it," he finished for her. He raised his hand at the protest he saw forming in her eyes. "Okay, I know. What you do with your future is none of my business. I'm just grateful you're here for Sarah now."

"You know I thought I didn't want to do this. But I'm glad it worked out."

He smiled, liking the way her lips curved softly when she thought of Sarah. "You're glad I didn't take no for an answer?"

"Well..." She looked up at him, laughter filling those green eyes. "I did think you were a tiny bit overpersistent."

"Who, me?" His eyebrows lifted. "I'm sure no one's ever said that about me before."

"Maybe they used the word *stubborn*," she suggested.

He lifted a hand to acknowledge the shot. "That might have been mentioned a time or two."

It suddenly occurred to him to wonder just what he was doing. He'd come out here to thank her for Sarah, hadn't he? This wasn't about Sarah. This was about the two of them.

He moved a step closer, and her uplifted face was inches from his. Flecks of gold glinted in her sea-green eyes, and her mouth...he'd been longing to kiss that mouth since the first time he saw her. He clasped her arms and drew her an inch nearer.

Her eyes darkened, and he heard her breath catch. His heart pounded in a way he hadn't felt in a very long time. He bent, and their lips were a breath apart.

Leigh's hands came up to touch his shirt tentatively. He felt the touch through the fabric, felt her breath, felt the warmth radiating from her skin. Then suddenly her face turned away.

He released her instantly and stepped back as the blood pounded in his head. What was he doing? He wasn't going to get involved with any woman, least of all a woman like Leigh, who would expect feelings he didn't have to give anymore.

"I'm sorry." Her voice shook just a bit.

He made an abrupt gesture with his hand. "No reason for you to be sorry. Just me. I don't know what I was thinking."

She lifted her face and met his eyes squarely. "We both know what, Daniel. And it wasn't just you. It was me, too." She took a deep breath. "But we also both know this would be a bad idea."

"Right. Absolutely. You're Sarah's teacher."

"And you're her father." She smiled fleetingly. "And my employer."

"Well." He didn't know whether to be glad or sorry that she'd drawn the lines so clearly. "Let's forget this happened. Deal?"

"Deal." Her smile might have faltered for an instant, and then she turned to the car. "I'd better get going."

"Right. I'll see you tomorrow." He hesitated. "We will see you tomorrow, won't we?"

"You can count on it." She slid into the seat. "Forget the last five minutes. They didn't happen." She pulled the door closed.

He nodded, raised his hand as she drove out. But he wasn't nodding in agreement, because he knew full well that he wasn't going to forget the last five minutes, not one second of it.

By the time she reached the house, Leigh told herself she was ready to forget all about what had happened. No, what hadn't happened. It hadn't.

Unfortunately, her lips still tingled as if it had, and Daniel's fresh, masculine scent seemed to linger, reminding her that she had nearly made a big mistake.

Unsuitable. If it had been unsuitable for her just to talk with Tommy's father about him, how much more unsuitable would it be to actually become involved with Daniel? Because that was what she'd been thinking; she couldn't deny it.

The two cases were nothing alike, some rebellious part of her mind argued. She was on her own now. She wasn't working for a school.

No, but she could get hurt just as badly. And there was Sarah to consider. All her energy, all her attention, had to be focused on doing the best for Sarah.

Besides, Daniel had made it clear he thought that what had almost happened was just as wrong as she did. He'd backed away so quickly she might have thought she'd imagined the whole thing.

She pulled into the driveway in a spray of crushed shells, parked, then yanked the parking brake on far harder than was necessary. No, she couldn't have thought she'd imagined it. Not at all.

Meggie and Mark hovered over a cardboard box on the deck. She got out, managing a smile for them. "Hey, kids. What's going on?"

"Shh!" Meggie put her finger to her lips.

"They're sleeping," she said in a loud stage whisper. "We don't want to wake them up."

"Jemima brought her kittens out," Mark explained.

Jemima, a gorgeous calico with an independent streak, had obviously had her kittens several weeks ago, but she'd kept them in hiding. Maybe she hadn't relished the attention Meggie was bound to pour on them.

Leigh knelt beside her niece and nephew, putting an arm around each of them. Five kittens curled up against Jemima. The cat looked up at Leigh, blinked slowly and then licked the nearest one.

"My, they're certainly colorful, aren't they?" Jemima had managed to produce two gray-striped babies, a black with white bib, an orange-and-white, and one lovely calico like herself.

"I think they're beautiful." Meggie extended a cautious finger toward the little calico kitten. Jemima hissed.

Leigh closed her hand over Meggie's. "Jemima's a good mother. She wants to protect her babies. Maybe we'd better let them sleep for now."

Meggie's lower lip came out. "But I want to hold one."

Leigh pulled Meggie around to face her. "Meggie, you wouldn't want to upset Jemima after she's had such wonderful babies, would you? She might take them into hiding again if you do."

Meggie pouted for another moment, then her usual sunny smile came out. "I'm going to tell Mommy that Jemima needs some extra milk tonight." She darted into the house, letting the door slam behind her.

Mark leaned against Leigh. "Know what, Aunt Leigh? My summer school started today."

"That's right, I'd forgotten that was today. How was it?" The elementary school ran a half-day enrichment program for six weeks during the summer, and both he and Meggie were attending.

"Great. We're going to do all kinds of neat science stuff, and maybe even learn French."

"That is great, Mark." Leigh put her arm around him, relishing the quiet moment. Mark didn't usually sit still long enough for hugs.

"I was thinking, maybe you could come to my school." Mark fixed those bright eyes of his on her face. "You could teach the kids sign language. Everybody wants to learn that."

Leigh's heart gave a lurch at the thought of her being back in a classroom again. Teaching Sarah was hard enough. Going back to a real school, being part of it even for a little while…it would just hurt too much.

"I don't think so, Mark. But thank you for asking me."

"But Aunt Leigh…"

Leigh tapped him on the nose. "You forget I'm teaching Sarah now during the day. I'm not free to go to your school."

"Oh." Mark pondered for a moment. "Maybe Sarah could come, too. She'd like that."

Maybe so, but she doubted that Daniel would. Anyway, Sarah wasn't ready for anything so formal, as much as it would do her good to be around other children.

"I don't think so, Mark."

"Well, then."

Mark's persistence reminded her of his mother.

"What about if you come to my Sunday-school class? You could do that, couldn't you?"

Leigh ruffled his hair. She didn't have another no in her. "Sure I could. If it's okay with your teacher."

Mark grinned. "It's okay. I already asked her."

"You monster." Leigh tickled him. "What made you so sure I'd say yes?"

"I just knew," Mark said between giggles. "Maybe Sarah could come to Sunday school."

"I don't think—" Leigh stopped. She'd been about to say she didn't think that would work, but why wouldn't it? One short hour of Sunday school, with Leigh right there for support and a small group of children, might be just what Sarah needed.

How might Daniel react to that idea? Leigh had no idea if Daniel even attended church. Jamie would probably know. In any event, she felt quite sure that the thought of taking Sarah to Sunday school had never crossed his mind.

Well, then, it was about to. Leigh stood up with sudden energy. It was a good idea, and if Daniel didn't think so, he'd find out that she could be just as stubborn as he was.

Chapter Six

As part of her plan to involve Sarah with other children, Leigh decided to take Meggie along to play the next day. The girls could have the morning together, then she'd run Meggie to the school enrichment program in the afternoon.

Meggie was delighted, of course. She raced into Sarah's room, chattering a mile a minute, and darted from toy to toy, exploring everything. Sarah hung back, obviously not knowing what to make of Meggie but with a glint of curiosity in her dark eyes.

"It's okay," Leigh said, signing. "Why don't you show Meggie your toys."

Hesitantly, Sarah opened the small cupboard that held her doll dishes, then pulled two chairs up to the table.

"Oh, good." Meggie began setting the table. "Look, this is how Mommy sets the table. Knives and forks go here. Auntie Leigh, we need napkins."

Trying to hide her smile, Leigh pulled tissues

from the box to serve as napkins. Meggie didn't know more than a few phrases in sign language, but that didn't stop her. She talked away, gesturing widely when she didn't know the signs, with none of the awkwardness an adult would have felt in this situation.

Sarah, shy at first, soon warmed up. How could anyone not warm up, in the face of Meggie's bubbling personality? And since Meggie talked enough for two, she wasn't bothered by Sarah's silences.

The only hitch came when Meggie approached the doll and the cradle. "The baby needs to get up to eat." She reached for the doll, only to have Sarah snatch it from her hands.

"No!" Sarah smoothed the blanket around the doll, holding it close. "Ba-by," she added, to Leigh's astonishment. Then she put the doll carefully back into the cradle.

Meggie never had been one to take no for an answer. She leaned against the cradle, putting her face close to Sarah's. "But the baby *needs* to get up," she wheedled. "Please?"

Sarah's lips closed in a firm line so like Daniel's it startled Leigh. She shook her head violently, her dark braids flying.

"But..."

Maybe it was time to intervene. "Why don't we go down to the beach," Leigh suggested. "Let's put our swimsuits on."

Clouds had begun to form on the horizon by the time the three of them approached the building project. Daniel glanced at them, hammer suspended momentarily.

"I see we have company today." He smiled at

Meggie, but when he looked at Leigh, his smile vanished. "Are you sure this is a good idea?" he said quietly.

For an instant Leigh's mind fled back to the day before, when he'd almost kissed her. Her cheeks flamed. Then she realized he was talking about Meggie.

"Meggie and Sarah are getting along fine." Her voice was stiff. "I wouldn't let anything happen."

"Hi, Sarah's daddy." Meggie moved a step closer, taking her welcome for granted. "What are you making?"

Leigh ruffled Meggie's short blond hair. "Mr. Gregory."

"'Daniel,'" Daniel corrected. He smiled at Meggie, and Leigh's tension eased. "I'm making a lodge, Meggie. What do you think of it?"

Meggie tipped her head to one side, considering. "It's not very pretty, is it?"

"Meggie!" Leigh found herself wishing Meggie didn't talk quite so much. Now, if she could divide her chatter with Sarah, for instance...

But Daniel just laughed. "Not pretty yet, no. But it will be when it's finished." He hefted the hammer. "So I'd better get back to work on it."

"I'd like to talk with you," Leigh said quickly, the Sunday-school idea in her mind. "Do you have a minute?"

He shook his head. "Not now." He gestured toward the clouds. "There's rain coming this afternoon. I can't stop now."

"Later, then?"

He sighed, elaborately. Obviously he found her

just as persistent as Meggie. "I'll join you on the beach a little later."

She had to be content with that for the moment. Gathering up towels and sand toys, she shooed the two girls down to the beach.

The tide was just going out, forming a new tidal pool. "Look, Sarah!" Meggie ran to it. "Look! We can find lots of things in the pool."

Meggie really was a daughter of the sea islands, Leigh realized. She knew far more about the creatures of the beach than Leigh did. She scooped up a handful of wet sand, sifting it knowledgeably.

"See?" She held out a handful of tiny shells, their colors making a rainbow in her small hand. "Coquina shells, Aunt Leigh. Tell Sarah what they are."

Since Leigh hadn't the faintest idea how to sign that, she settled for "pretty shells," which seemed to please Sarah. Sarah followed Meggie's actions, acquiring her own handful of shells, which she deposited in a careful pile on Leigh's towel.

Leigh grinned. Whether he knew it or not, Daniel was shortly going to have a house decorated with all the things Sarah couldn't bear to leave behind on the beach. Beachcomber's disease, Jamie called it. She sorted through her children's treasures every few days, getting rid of anything that had started to smell.

Leigh scavenged through the tidal pool with Sarah and Meggie, but Daniel's face, intent as he worked, insisted on invading her thoughts. She understood his passion to finish the project—at least, she thought she did. He believed it was the only way to provide the best for Sarah. And he'd work himself half to death, if necessary, to do that. She couldn't help admiring his single-minded determination, even while she doubted his aims.

He'd as much as told her that he felt responsible for the failure of his marriage. Maybe that was why he'd backed off so quickly the day before. And for Sarah? How much guilt did he hold over her situation? Maybe he thought he should have fought to keep Sarah with him. If only she knew exactly where those guilt feelings came from, then maybe she'd know how to convince him to take a second look at his plans for Sarah. But she doubted she'd ever get close enough to learn that.

Her face flushed as she pictured that moment the day before when they'd been close—too close. Daniel had known that was a mistake just as much as she had. Maybe his reluctance to stop long enough for a conversation now had something to do with that.

The girls, tiring of the tidal pool at last, began a sand construction.

"A lodge," Meggie insisted. "We have to make a lodge, just like Sarah's daddy's."

"Good idea." Leigh signed Meggie's plan to Sarah, who nodded, then picked up her sand shovel.

Leigh settled on her towel and left them to it. She watched, fascinated by the interaction between the two of them. Meggie bossed, of course. She couldn't help herself. But Sarah dug in her heels a time or two, flatly refusing to go down to the waves for a pail of water. Leigh grinned as Meggie tried orders, then cajoling, head tipped to the side in the method that usually melted her daddy's heart.

It didn't work with Sarah. She shook her head firmly and shoved the pail into Meggie's hands.

Meggie grabbed it and stomped down to do it herself.

"What's so funny?"

Leigh jerked, startled. She hadn't heard Daniel's approach, and suddenly there he was, dropping to the sand next to her.

"The girls," she said, nodding at them. "Sarah just stood up to Meggie."

"And that's good?"

"You bet it is." Leigh smiled. "That's very good, for both of them."

Daniel's arm brushed hers as he leaned forward, watching the children. Her skin tingled from the brief contact.

"What are they making?"

"A lodge. You inspired them."

He leaned back on one elbow, stretching long legs out in front of him. "I hope mine's got better underpinnings than theirs does, or it will wash out to sea with the next tide." He nodded toward the thickening clouds. "Or with the rain."

A house built on sand... Probably he wouldn't appreciate the comparison.

"I'm sure it does," she murmured.

Daniel focused his gaze on her face. "You wanted to talk to me. Something about Sarah."

Sarah, Sunday school, the value of being around other kids. How to convince him?

"Sarah really seems to enjoy being with Meggie," she began.

He frowned, watching the children. "Sarah acts

as though she understands what Meggie's saying. That's impossible."

"We're seeing it, so I guess it's not impossible." Why was he so reluctant to believe the evidence of his own eyes? "I think it's a combination of things…a little lipreading, some faint hearing, a lot of gestures. And maybe just the novelty of being with another child. It's making her try harder."

"I never thought…" Daniel's frown deepened. "Judith insisted Meggie should be protected from other children. She thought she'd get hurt."

Leigh would like to have a few words with Judith on that subject, but it seemed unlikely that would ever happen.

"It's certainly possible that Sarah's feelings would be hurt by other children," she said carefully. "But that happens to all kids."

"It's not the same thing."

"Meggie came home crying the other day because one of her playmates called her a silly baby. She sobbed, swore vengeance, declared she'd never speak to her again. The next day they were best friends once more."

"Sarah's not like Meggie." His tone hardened.

"They're more alike than different." Maybe she'd better get to the point, before she alienated him entirely. "Anyway, I think exposure to other children would be good for Sarah. Just a few kids, in a controlled setting."

He looked at her, but his face didn't give anything away. "What setting?"

She took a deep breath. "I'd like to take Sarah to Sunday school with Meggie and Mark."

"No." His reply was instantaneous. "I don't want that."

"I really think it would be good for her. And there aren't that many children in the class—maybe eight or ten. I'd stay with her every minute."

She sounded like Meggie, wheedling her way into something. But this was so important. Why couldn't he see that?

Daniel got that harassed look that said she was pushing too hard. "But Sunday school... Look, I don't go to church all that much myself."

She didn't think she could ask him why. This was like treading through a minefield, never knowing what might blow up.

"I'm not trying to convert you, Daniel. Or Sarah. I just think the experience would be good for her."

He frowned, the strong planes of his face growing rigid. "When Sarah was a baby, when we first started to think something was wrong..." He stopped, swallowed hard.

"You feel God let you down," she said softly, her heart hurting for him. Without thinking, she put her hand over his. He turned his hand, and their palms touched.

Warmth radiated from his skin. She wanted to look away from him, to pull her hand away, but she couldn't seem to do it.

His eyes grew darker, and fine lines fanned out from them. "I decided a long time ago that I couldn't depend on anyone or anything else. Just myself. And I'm all Sarah can depend on now."

No one could rely only on himself. Not even a person as strong as Daniel. But he wasn't ready to hear that from her. She'd have to try to show him another way.

"Does that really mean Sarah shouldn't go to Sunday school? Does it mean she should pass up something that might be good for her?"

His face closed, shutting her out. "I don't want Sarah thinking she can rely on God answering her prayers. Or on other people. Sorry if that offends you, but that's how it is."

"I'm not offended." How could she be offended? At least he'd been honest with her, even if it wasn't what she wanted to hear. "I'm just sorry."

"Auntie Leigh!" Meggie jumped up and down, holding both hands wide. "It's starting to rain!"

Leigh scrambled to her feet. "Well, you're already wet, aren't you? But I guess we'd better get up to the house. We have to get you ready for school."

Daniel joined her in gathering up towels and sand buckets, then took Sarah's hand. "Come on, sugar. Let's run for it."

Sarah trotted up the path beside him, and Leigh followed with Meggie. The wind caught at her T-shirt, billowing it around her legs, and fat wet drops spattered her. They seemed to echo the tears she felt inside for Daniel, for Sarah.

When they reached the house, Daniel let Leigh take over getting the two children dried and changed. The spicy aroma of chili drew him to the kitchen, where Joe was stirring the contents of a cast-iron kettle with his longest wooden spoon.

Daniel leaned on the counter. "You making enough for the whole island?"

"Never made a little batch of chili in my life. I wouldn't know how." Joe sent a glance over his shoulder and seemed to assess his mood. "What's wrong with you? The rain? Or the woman?"

Daniel shrugged, crossing the room to stare out the window. Rain battered the carpet of pine needles, and wind set the tops of the palmettos tossing. "Maybe a little of both."

"Can't do much about the rain." Joe tapped his spoon on the edge of the kettle and set it down. "What's Leigh want now?"

Daniel felt himself tense. Joe would probably agree with Leigh on this one. "She wants to take Sarah to Sunday school with her niece and nephew."

"Don't see anything so wrong with that."

"You know how I feel about it. And Sarah's my daughter, remember? I make the decisions." True enough. So why did he feel this defensive?

Joe didn't argue, just stared at him with those wise, ageless dark eyes.

"You thinking about Sarah now? Or yourself?"

The old man knew him, all right. There wasn't any answer that wouldn't expose too much of what he felt. So he turned and left the kitchen.

He'd intended to go into the cubbyhole that served as his office, try to make some sense of the books. But the sound of giggles drew him irresistibly up the stairs.

He ought to stay away from Leigh Christopher, with her warm heart and her laughing eyes. She challenged him in ways he didn't want to think about, not again. And she'd all but told him she thought he was wrong, maybe even selfish, about Sarah.

She'd known Sarah for a couple of days only. What right did she have, acting as if she had all the answers? He was Sarah's father.

The militant mood lasted until he stood in the doorway of Sarah's room, watching.

Leigh had obviously been up to her elbows in wet little people. Her shorts and T-shirt were splashed, and even the bangs that framed her face looked damp. She was drying Meggie's hair with a towel—something that seemed to have turned into a giggling wrestling match.

Sarah looked on, a wistful expression on her face. Before he could take a step toward her, Leigh had turned and swept her into the struggle. For an instant Sarah stiffened, then she smiled and tossed a towel over Meggie's head.

Something seemed to clutch at his heart. Sarah smiling, playing just like any other child. He'd never seen that before. Maybe he'd never thought to see it. Sarah had always seemed so contained, so solemn. Ashley and her family had considered that normal. Maybe they'd been wrong.

Leigh spotted him then, and her face stilled as their eyes met. If she thought he was angry, she'd wandered far from the truth.

"Seems like fun."

She smiled, face relaxing. "Fun, maybe, but how we'll ever get Meggie ready for school on time at this rate, I don't know." She plopped both girls down on the bed with a fresh towel each. "Now, dry that hair, okay?"

"Looks like you need more dried than they do."
He glanced at her wet clothing.

She grimaced, waving the tail of her oversize
T-shirt as if to air-dry it. "Comes with the territory.
I never managed to arrive home from school with-
out at least one major clothing repair to do."

"Maybe you should get some coveralls. And
work boots." He resisted the temptation to brush
back the damp hair from her forehead.

"A suit of armor would be more like it." She
glanced toward the two girls, now drying each
other's hair, and her smile faded. "May I ask you
something?"

He shrugged. "Sure."

"Why doesn't Sarah think she's pretty?"

He felt as though she'd slammed him in the stomach. "What makes you think that?"

"Yesterday." Her eyes were troubled. "I signed
'pretty girl' when we looked in the mirror." Her
hand made a circle around her face. "She got upset.
She wouldn't let me say that about her. I thought
you might know what gave her that idea."

His jaw was so tight he had to force the words
out. "She didn't get it from me—that's for sure. I
suppose Ashley…" He stopped, not wanting to go
on. But that concern in Leigh's green eyes was for
his child. "Ashley was a beautiful woman. Appearance meant a lot to her. I suppose she might,
without meaning to, have given Sarah the idea she
wasn't pretty."

Leigh's eyes were bright with what might have
been tears, but her voice sounded deliberately casual. "That happens, I guess. No matter how well-

intentioned people are, kids sometimes come up with wrong ideas.''

This was about as wrong as it could be. The idea that his sweet, lovely Sarah didn't think she was pretty cut him as deep as anything could. His hands clenched into fists, and he forced them to relax.

''So what can we do about it?''

''I'm not sure.''

Leigh glanced toward the two girls, and he followed her gaze. They were in front of the mirror now. Sarah watched in apparent fascination as Meggie inexpertly brushed the short blond hair around her face.

''Aunt Leigh,'' she called. ''You'll have to do Sarah's hair. I don't know how to make braids.''

''I'll take care of it.''

As Leigh went back to the children, an idea blossomed in Daniel's mind. Maybe, just maybe, he knew something that would help.

After lunch, he insisted on driving them to drop Meggie at her school. He saw Sarah, face pressed against the glass, watch Meggie run through the puddles into the school.

His heart hurt again. He wanted so much for his daughter, but whatever he gave, it wouldn't be enough to make up for what she didn't have.

He drove slowly back down the main street of the village and pulled into a parking place in front of the general store.

Leigh looked at him, a question in her eyes. ''Are we doing some shopping?''

''Not exactly.'' He hesitated. How sure was he that this was a good idea? Probably not very, but he was going to try it anyway. "I thought we might make another stop." He nodded. "At the beautician's."

Leigh's hand went to her hair and she smiled. "Do you think I need some help?"

"I think you look great just the way you are." That came out a little more warmly than he'd intended. He turned in his seat to see Sarah. "Sarah really seemed to like Meggie's short hair. And yours. I thought we'd ask if she'd like a haircut."

Pleasure shone from Leigh's eyes. "Daniel, what a great idea."

He shrugged, feeling ridiculously pleased at her approval. "It's worth a try."

Leigh turned to Sarah, her hands flying. "Sarah, would you like to get your hair cut? Short, like Meggie's?"

Sarah put both hands on her braids. She seemed a little scared at the prospect. He could see her eyes study her reflection in the rearview mirror. Then, slowly, she nodded.

A dozen times in the next half hour he thought Sarah would back out. Or he would. The perfumed atmosphere of the beauty shop had him itching to get back outside again.

For Sarah, he reminded himself. *You'd do a lot more to make her happy.*

The beautician snipped and chatted and studied the results. Leigh encouraged and distracted. Finally the woman sighed and put down her scissors.

"Perfect," she said. She spun the chair around so Sarah could see herself in the mirror. "It's just perfect."

Sarah's hair swirled, dark and shiny, close around

her face like a cap. Her tiny face appeared rounder; her brown eyes, bigger. He loved it, but more important was what Sarah would think. He smiled at her solemn reflection in the mirror.

Sarah leaned forward slowly, looking at herself. Then she leaned back again. She tipped her head to the side. Then she smiled, pointing. Slowly, with great deliberation, she brought her hand up in the gesture he'd seen Leigh make.

Pretty girl.

For a moment his vision blurred as he blinked back tears. "That's right, Sarah. Pretty girl." He glanced at Leigh, to find that her eyes were bright with unshed tears, too. "Pretty girl."

Chapter Seven

It was a triumph to celebrate, Leigh thought, swinging Sarah's hand in hers as they walked back into the house. To have Sarah show happiness in her appearance thrilled her. The fact that it came through Daniel's involvement was the icing on the cake.

Joe came out of the living room, dust cloth in hand, as they walked into the hall. Sarah ran to him, pirouetting to show off her new haircut.

"My, oh, my!" Joe clapped. "Is that our Miss Sarah?"

Sarah smiled and twirled around again. Leigh looked at Daniel. She'd never seen his face so relaxed, never seen so much love shining from his eyes. Her throat tightened. He resembled the younger Daniel in the picture he'd shown her, holding a chubby baby…the Daniel whose life had still been intact.

"Well." She eyed her watch and cleared her throat. "I guess it's about time for me to leave."

"Don't go." Daniel glanced from her to Sarah, still

smiling. "We have to celebrate. Stay for supper, and we'll order in a pizza."

"What about..." She turned to Joe and realized he wore an elderly navy jacket over his usual white shirt and bow tie.

"This is Joe's big night out," Daniel said, a teasing note in his voice. "He's going to flutter the ladies' hearts."

Joe sent him a reproving look. He tucked the dust cloth in his cleaning basket. "I'm going to evening prayer service," he said. Then his eyes twinkled. "I can't help it if the ladies enjoy having a handsome man to help with the praying." He consulted his pocket watch. "I best be off."

He blew a kiss to Sarah. She solemnly returned it, and he went out.

"We're on our own, so this would be a good time to start those signing lessons you promised me. Remember?" Daniel picked up the phone. "How about it? Mushrooms? Pepperoni? Anchovies?"

Spending the evening within range of that high-voltage smile probably wasn't the smartest thing she'd ever done.

"Anything but anchovies," she said.

"You've got it." He dialed. "Enjoy it. We've had a pizzeria on the island for only the last two years."

She let her eyes widen. "How did you survive without pizza?"

"We had to improvise." He gave her a mischievous grin.

Daniel turned to the receiver to place the order, and she tried to convince her heart to stop thumping.

By the time they were halfway through the pizza, Leigh realized her apprehensions had been correct.

Daniel, busy and distracted, was attractive enough. Daniel relaxed and smiling, his arm brushing hers as he reached across the kitchen table for another piece of pizza, was...overpowering.

This is a business relationship, she reminded herself. *You don't want anything else, and neither does he.*

But it was hard to keep that in mind when she was surrounded by the warmth and laughter of two people she'd begun to care for too much. It would be so easy to want to become a real part of this...so easy that it scared her.

"No more for me." She shook her head when Daniel pushed the pizza box toward her one more time. "Maybe we ought to start the signing lesson before Sarah gets too tired."

"Sarah?" Daniel's dark brows lifted.

"It'll be good for her to help you with your signing." That came out sounding a little too flurried. "It'll help her, too."

If he recognized that she was using Sarah as a buffer against being alone with him, he didn't show it. "Okay, let's get started." He moved the pizza box to the counter, then swung his chair to face hers. Their knees almost touched. "What first, Teacher?"

Leigh quickly pulled Sarah's chair around so that the three of them sat facing one another in a tight little circle. "Help Daddy sign, okay?"

Sarah nodded. "Okay," she signed.

Deciding not to assume anything about how much he had learned or remembered, Leigh started with the basics: facial expression, pronouns, simple sentences.

Sarah loved it. That was the most astonishing thing. The child whose face had seemed a closed book just a few days ago blossomed with pleasure. When Daniel mastered the fist to his forehead for *stupid* and used it when he made a mistake, she began to giggle.

The sound, so like Meggie's, touched Leigh's heart. Daniel's, too, she realized, because he did it again and again.

"You're doing that just to hear her laugh," she said softly.

Daniel leaned forward so that their knees touched. "Do you blame me?"

She shook her head. "No. How could I?" She turned at the touch of Sarah's hand. "Sarah wants you to learn *I'm happy.*" She demonstrated, and he followed her movements, hand circling outward from his heart. "Perfect."

His eyebrows lifted in the classic question mode. "You happy?" he signed.

She couldn't manage to look away, and she suspected happiness was written all over her face, needing no interpretation. "I'm happy."

Daniel smiled slowly. He put his hand over hers, and she seemed to feel his heart beating through the touch of his palm. For a long moment she couldn't say anything...because anything she said would reveal too much, would involve her too deeply.

Sarah plopped her little hand down on theirs. Startled, Leigh turned to her.

"I'm sleepy," Sarah signed, fingers drawing down from her face. "Sleep-y," she added aloud, carefully.

"Good talking, Sarah." Leigh drew her hand from Daniel's.

"We'd better get you to bed." Daniel lifted Sarah in his arms, then peered over her head at Leigh. "Thanks for the lesson, Leigh. I'll look forward to the next one." His deep voice seemed to lend the words a little extra emphasis.

"Oh, wait, I have something for Sarah." Leigh grabbed the seashell night-light from her bag and held it out to the child. "I got this for you. I thought it might make you sleep better."

"You mean without a lamp on." Daniel sounded resigned. "Believe me, Leigh, I've tried everything."

She should have realized he'd thought of that already. "Sometimes a special night-light helps." She smiled. "I used to have a teddy bear one that kept the dark away. But Meggie has one like this. She thought you'd like it."

"Thank you," Sarah signed.

But Leigh could read the reservation in her eyes. "It's okay." She patted Sarah's hand. "You can have the lamp on, too, if you want."

"Let's give it a try." Daniel hoisted Sarah a bit higher and smiled at Leigh. "But you'll have to stay through bedtime if you want to find out."

With Sarah watching her, she couldn't say no. "I'll clean up down here while you get Sarah ready for bed."

"You don't have to do that."

She picked up the pizza box. "We can't leave a mess for Joe. He might not let us order pizza again." And helping Daniel get his daughter ready for bed was just too intimate, too much a family thing. She didn't want to start liking a role she could never fill.

There wasn't much cleaning up to do, but Leigh stretched it out until she heard Daniel call her.

Upstairs, Sarah was already tucked into her bed. Daniel sat next to her. He looked at Leigh, eyebrows lifted. "We thought we'd let you turn the new night-light on."

Leigh took the seashell and pressed it into the outlet. The gentle glow turned the shell translucent.

Sarah's eyes widened. "Pretty," she signed.

"Yes. Pretty," Daniel said, but he looked at Leigh instead of the night-light.

"Good night, Sarah." Leigh leaned over for a good-night hug. "Can we turn the lamp off?"

Sarah hesitated for a moment, then she nodded. Daniel reached over and switched it off, then kissed her.

"Good night, pretty girl." His voice was a soft drawl that touched Leigh's heart.

Daniel followed Leigh into the hallway. After pulling the door half-closed behind him, he paused, listening, then he moved away from the door.

"So far, so good. That was a kind thought, Leigh. The night-light, I mean." He took a step closer, reaching out as if to touch her. His eyes appeared very dark in the dimly lit hallway.

"It was nothing." The words seemed to have gotten lodged in her throat somewhere, and they came out sounding breathless. "You're the one who did everything today. The haircut, the pizza— I've never seen Sarah so happy."

"How about Leigh?" He brushed a strand of hair from her cheek. The touch of his fingers warmed her skin and set her heart pumping faster. "Are you happy?"

She gazed up at him. His mouth was a breath away from hers. If he moved...if she moved...

Sarah cried out.

Daniel swung away instantly. He was back in the

room before Leigh could take a step. She followed, more slowly, disappointment seeping into her. Apparently her good idea wasn't good enough.

Daniel switched on the lamp, and Sarah's sobs stopped.

"It's okay, sweetheart." He patted her. "It's okay. You can have the lamp on if you want."

Sarah nodded vigorously, then looked at Leigh.

"It's all right." Leigh smiled. "You can still use your new light, too."

Nodding, Sarah slid back down beneath the covers. She watched as Daniel adjusted the shade on the lamp, and then she closed her eyes, still holding his hand.

"I'll say good-night," Leigh murmured.

She went back down the stairs, trying to swallow her disappointment. All right, it hadn't worked. That was no reason to berate herself. She couldn't expect to solve all Sarah's problems in a few days.

She'd reached the porch, when she heard Daniel coming after her. She paused, waiting for him. Maybe she owed him an "I told you so."

He came onto the porch and let the screen door close behind him. Night sounds—tree frogs, crickets, an owl off hunting—filled the air.

"Sorry," she said before he could speak. "I guess I was wrong." Her voice showed a ridiculous tendency to wobble.

"It's not your fault." He moved nearer, then gestured back toward the lit hallway. "I don't want to go out of earshot, but I wanted to say—"

"I told you so?" She tried to keep it light.

"No." His hand closed warmly on her arm. "I

wanted to say thanks. Hey, you tried. It was a good thought. Sarah just wasn't ready yet.''

"I know." She glanced up, but the darkness hid his face. "I tried to do too much, too soon." She shrugged. "You'll have noticed I tend to be a little impulsive."

"I've noticed you have a kind heart." There was a smile in his voice. "So, do you still want to take Sarah to Sunday school?"

For a moment she didn't understand, and then happiness flooded through her. "Do you mean it? But why? I thought you didn't want that for her."

He shrugged, and she thought she sensed discomfort in the movement. "Maybe I spoke too soon when I said no. Or maybe I was thinking of myself instead of Sarah. Anyway, you can take her, if you still think it'll do her good."

"Thank you, Daniel." Impulsively, she reached toward him. "You won't regret it."

Her hand touched his shoulder. She felt strong muscles, warm skin through the thin cotton of his shirt. Her mouth abruptly lost the ability to form words. She tried to snatch away her hand, but his covered it, pressing her palm flat against his chest.

She could feel his heart beat. Or was that hers pounding in her ears? Daniel reached out, caressing her cheek. He tipped her face up toward his. His mouth, warm, almost tentative at first, found hers. Then his arms went around her and his embrace wasn't tentative at all.

Dizzying moments later, Leigh pulled away from him. "I..." This wasn't a good idea, she wanted to say. We should be rational. We... "Good night." She turned and fled to her car.

* * *

Daniel frowned as he turned down the lane to Josh and Jamie's house Sunday afternoon. This was not what he'd intended to be doing today. He had too much work to finish on the building, and who knew how long the good weather would last? He shouldn't be wasting a sunny afternoon this way.

But he was. Blame it on Jamie. She'd called, determined that he'd share Sunday dinner with them after church. After all, he'd be coming anyway to pick up Sarah, and the least they could do was feed him.

His protests—that he didn't have time, that having him for dinner was an imposition, that he had too much work to do—just rolled right off her. She kept on talking, and in the end he'd given in because it was too hard to keep saying no. He grinned ruefully. The women in that family just had too much persistence.

Shells crunched under his tires as he pulled in by the house. And if he was honest, he'd have to admit to another reason for coming...to see Leigh.

Not that he hadn't seen her, of course. She'd been in his house every day, teaching Sarah, winning over Joe, filling the old place with laughter. But with him she'd been evasive. She'd avoided every opportunity to be alone with him, until he'd finally gotten the message. That kiss had been a big mistake.

Well, he'd known that. Probably knew it the minute it happened, and just couldn't stop himself. Her lips had been so inviting, the touch of her hand so appealing, that he'd given in to the feeling he'd harbored since the first moment he saw her.

Mistake, big mistake. Leigh had agreed to teach Sarah; that was all. She clearly didn't want a relationship with him. And even if she did, even if he built too much on her sweet response in the moments she'd been in his arms...well, it was still a mistake.

Leigh Christopher wasn't a woman who'd settle for less than a complete commitment from a man. She'd want forever. She'd want what he didn't have to give anymore.

So he wouldn't kiss her. He'd try to rebuild the friendship that had started between them, but he wouldn't kiss her. No matter how difficult it was.

Sarah came running to meet him the moment he got out of the car. The smile she wore as she threw her arms around him spoke volumes. He peered over her head at Leigh, who looked as cool as a tall glass of water in a green-and-white sundress.

"Hey, Leigh. I guess it went well."

Her smile was a little cautious. "Sarah had a good time, I think. She liked being with the other kids."

He caressed his daughter's cap of dark hair. "And the other kids? How were they?" Did they tease her, pity her? That was what he really wanted to ask, but he couldn't seem to.

"They got along fine." Leigh's eyes said she knew exactly what he was thinking. "Hearing kids are usually so fascinated by sign language that it bridges any awkwardness. We had a great time, really."

She was reassuring him as if he were the five-year-old. He ought to resent it, but he didn't. "I'm glad."

Her smile lost that note of caution. "Good." She gestured toward the deck. "Come join the gang. Jamie's fixed a ton of food, so I hope you're hungry."

In a moment or two she had Sarah and Meggie involved in setting the picnic table, so he wandered over to the grill, where Josh was flipping burgers.

"You in charge of the cooking?"

Josh grinned. "Don't look so nervous. Jamie doesn't let me do anything I might mess up."

Daniel took the cold soda Josh handed him. "She thinks you can be left alone with the burgers?"

"Kid stuff." Josh slid a burger onto a roll. "I mean it. I've got a basket of fresh shrimp to do for the grown-ups, but we'll get the kids started first." He pointed. "You want to hand me those?"

They fell into a routine, with him filling the grill basket with shrimp and Josh splashing on the butter. It was surprising how long it had been since he'd done something so simple and companionable.

How long had it been since he'd bothered to socialize with his neighbors? In the first months after Ashley left, people had invited him out, had tried, however awkwardly, to sympathize.

That had been more painful than indifference. Finally he'd turned down every invitation, holing up with his pain and humiliation. After a while, people stopped asking.

And then when Sarah had come back, he'd been more anxious than ever to avoid company, afraid of putting her in a situation that would upset her. Maybe afraid of how people would react to her.

He glanced at Josh, who was turning away from the grill to assure his son the food would be ready in a minute. Josh wasn't offering any unwelcome sympathy. He was just being himself.

"Come and get it," Jamie called. "Before these ravenous kids eat it all."

"The Atlanta Falcons couldn't eat all this." Daniel slid onto the picnic bench next to Sarah.

Leigh landed a bowl of potato salad in front of him, then found a seat on the opposite side. Okay, so she didn't want to sit next to him. At least with her across from him, he could enjoy the view.

Jamie came to a halt at the table and frowned at Leigh. "What are you doing over there all by yourself?"

"Eating." Leigh gave her a look that should have stopped a charging gator but didn't seem to faze Jamie. "Aren't you going to sit down?" *And be quiet,* her tone seemed to add.

Josh cleared his throat. "Let's ask the blessing before the kids eat everything in sight."

Daniel bowed his head, noting that Sarah did the same without any prompting. She folded her hands gravely, just as Meggie did.

His heart clenched. There had been a time when this picture was how he'd envisioned their lives. But that wasn't how it had turned out.

Food sailed around the table as easily as the conversation. Jamie and Meggie each talked enough for two, and even eating didn't slow down the chatter. It took a while for him to realize that Leigh was signing what they said for Sarah.

She was making sure Sarah wouldn't feel left out. That was what Leigh had been trying to tell him that first day when she'd pitched into him about not signing enough. He looked at Sarah, saw the animation on her little face as she responded, saw the easy way Leigh's family acted with her.

His heart clenched again. If he could keep that happiness on his daughter's face always...

But that was impossible. Sooner or later life would slap her down. And when it did, he wasn't sure how he'd cope with that.

The adults lingered over coffee and pecan pie,

while the children ran off to play. Josh groaned and stretched.

"I'm going to have to get bigger pants if you keep feeding me like this, woman. I don't know how those kids can run around. All I'm fit for is a nap."

"Nobody told you to eat a second piece of pie." Jamie leaned across to refill his coffee cup, and Leigh grinned at Daniel behind her back. Obviously this was an old story.

Sarah ran out of the house and held something out to him. Daniel took the small picture. "What's this?"

"My picture," Sarah signed.

He glanced across at Leigh, raising his eyebrows.

"The Sunday-school teacher gave each child a picture of Jesus and the children. So they'd remember the story she told them. It glows in the dark." She held up her hand. "I didn't set that up, honest."

"I didn't say a word." He turned to Sarah and stroked her hair. "It's a lovely picture, honey. We'll put it in your room."

Sarah nodded. She leaned her head against his arm, tracing the figures in the picture with one small finger. Then Mark and Meggie dragged a basket onto the deck between them, and she ran off to join them.

He grinned at Leigh. "So it was just a coincidence, huh?"

She smiled back, and he had a feeling it was the first time she'd really been at ease with him since that kiss. "A coincidence," she said firmly.

"Dad-dy!"

The sound of Sarah verbalizing was startling enough to spin him around on the bench. "What is it, honey?"

She reached into the basket and came up with a

small orange-and-white ball of fluff. "Mine," she announced.

Daniel stared, horrified, at the kitten. "Sarah, I don't think…"

Meggie patted the kitten, then Sarah. "I gave it to her, Sarah's daddy. Mommy says we can keep two kittens only, so I gave that one to Sarah. It's my second favorite."

Both girls advanced on him, kitten held between them. He sent an accusing look at Leigh. Smiling, she rounded the table and sat down next to him. She let Sarah put the kitten in her lap.

"You have to ask Sarah's daddy first, Meggie. You know that's what Mommy said."

"Well, I am asking." Meggie leaned against his knee and peered up into his face, her blue eyes wide and innocent. "Can I give Sarah a kitten, please? She'll love it and take good care of it."

He sent another exasperated glance at Leigh, but she just looked down at the kitten, stroking it, then showing Sarah how to tickle under its chin.

The kitten started to purr under her hand. She obviously felt that, and her face lit with wonder. The expression grabbed him, wouldn't let go.

Meggie patted his arm, as if he were the kitten. "Please, Sarah's daddy? Please? She loves it a lot."

The last thing on earth they needed was a kitten. "Meggie, I…" He stopped. Three pairs of eyes were fixed on him. The kitten was the only one not staring at him. It was too busy snuggling against Leigh's chin. He lifted an eyebrow at Leigh. "She's not going to give up, is she?"

Leigh smiled. "It's a family trait."

"So I see." He ruffled the kitten's fur, his fingers

brushing Leigh's. Her cheeks got a little pinker, but she didn't pull away.

"Well, then." He cleared his throat. "I guess we have a kitten."

Chapter Eight

"Say it, Sarah." Leigh held up the flash card with
the picture of a cat. "You can do it."

On the other side of the kitchen table, Sarah
pouted. She folded her arms across her chest.

Leigh couldn't stop a smile. Even that small rebellious act was pure pleasure, because it showed Sarah's
growing confidence. Leigh glanced at the clock. Another few minutes and she'd call it quits with the flash
cards. It was nearly lunchtime anyway.

"Come on," she coaxed. "Say it." She signed the
tug on imaginary whiskers that meant *cat*.

Sarah glanced at the orange-and-white kitten,
which was curled up in its basket by the stove. Then
she gave Leigh a mischievous grin.

"Sas-sy!" she shouted, pointing to the kitten.

Joe's chuckle punctuated Leigh's laughter.

"All right, you win." She slid the cards into their
box. "It must be time for lunch, no?"

Joe handed her three plates, and she scooped the

cards to the end of the table. She set the places quickly, frowning, and glanced at Joe.

"Isn't Daniel coming in for lunch?"

He shook his head, ladling corn chowder into bowls. "Said he'd work straight through and just grab a sandwich later. Said he's worried about the weather."

Leigh looked out the window at a cloudless sky. "What's wrong with the weather?"

"Whole string of clear days, no rain in sight this time of year? Means a bad one coming before too long."

Leigh grinned. "Is that a bit of folk wisdom, or have you been watching the weather channel again?"

"I know what these old bones tell me." He kept a straight face, but the twinkle in his eyes gave him away. "And what the weather service has to say about storms in the Caribbean."

Leigh set a bowl of soup in front of Sarah. Maybe Daniel's obsession with getting as much work done as possible before the weather turned was understandable, but she'd barely seen him all week.

More important, she told herself sternly, was the fact that Sarah had barely seen him. He was at the construction site before his daughter woke up in the morning, and he stayed until Joe left after supper. He couldn't keep up that pace forever; no one could.

Sarah pushed her soup away fretfully. She frowned at Daniel's empty chair. The small gesture galvanized something in Leigh. If Daniel didn't recognize what he was doing, she'd have to tell him.

"I'm going down to the site. Maybe I can talk him into coming up long enough to eat, at least."

Joe looked doubtful. "You can try, I reckon."

The moment she stepped outside, the heat and humidity settled over her like a wet wool blanket. How could anyone work outside all day in this heat? Maybe islanders were born used to it.

The path down to the construction site was familiar territory by now. She came out of the trees, and the offshore breeze that accompanied the rising tide fluttered her shirt, cooling her.

She stopped long enough to shake sand from her sandals, then picked her way to the ladder Daniel had propped against the building.

"Daniel?"

He stopped, hammer in hand, and looked down at her. He'd shed his shirt, and his skin gleamed with perspiration. "What's wrong?"

"Nothing." Everything. "Can't you take a break now? I think Sarah would enjoy having lunch with you."

"Not now. I'll catch up with her tonight."

When you're too tired to give her the attention she craves from you. "Daniel, please come down for a minute. I need to talk to you, and this is giving me a stiff neck."

For a moment she thought he'd refuse. Then he sighed, put down the hammer and dropped to the sand. "Well?"

"Don't you want to get a drink while we talk?" She gestured toward the water jug, stowed in what little shade there was.

He frowned, but he walked to the jug, poured himself a cupful and drained it in one long gulp. She'd better use the time to figure out how she was going to say what she wanted to say, rather than watching the muscles in his neck work as he swallowed.

"Okay." He took another cupful and splashed it over his head. The droplets ran down his skin like rain down a windowpane, glistening where the light hit. "What's up?"

Leigh swallowed hard. Maybe she herself could use a drink of water. "I'm a little concerned about Sarah," she said carefully. "You haven't been spending much time with her. She misses you."

"She has you. Joe. That…that…kitten."

Leigh smiled. She'd already heard from Joe about Daniel accidentally shutting the kitten into the closet, only to be wakened in the middle of the night by outraged yowls.

"Of course she has us, but it's not the same. You're the one she loves. Depends on."

His mouth tightened. "That doesn't mean I can spend every minute with her."

"Every minute? How many minutes have you spent with her this week?"

Daniel planted his hands on his hips, glowering. She braced herself, expecting an explosion.

Then he took her arm and turned her toward the construction site. "What do you see?"

The unexpected touch dried her mouth, and she had to clear her throat before she answered. "I see you're making progress." She wasn't sure what kind of answer he looked for.

He shrugged. "Not enough. But that's not what I mean. When I see those eight half-finished rooms, I see Sarah's future."

"Daniel, I know you want to provide for her…"

"Have you looked out in the sound lately?" he demanded. "The bridge is coming. They say now it will be open by spring. I have to be ready." He frowned. "Some big hotel corporation just made an offer on Ted Summers's place down at the landing."

"But what does that have to do with Sarah?"

"Don't you understand?" His grip tightened. "Change is coming, ready or not. Either we prepare or we're forced out. It's happened on other islands. I can't let it happen to me. I'm all Sarah's got."

The passion in his voice, his eyes, almost deflected her. Almost.

"I know it's important, for you and for Sarah. But don't you understand? She needs you now. She doesn't comprehend all this." She waved her hand at the construction. She didn't want to make him angry, but she had to make him understand. "She just wants to be with her daddy."

"Look, I'm doing what's best, okay? Maybe you can help her understand that."

"That's a pretty big order for a five-year-old."

His mouth tightened, a small muscle in his jaw twitching. "I have to get back to work. Is that it?"

"Not quite." She got a frown for her effort. Well, she'd say what she intended to, regardless. "Sarah and I are planning something special tonight. To celebrate her not being afraid of the dark anymore."

He had the grace to look a little embarrassed. "You heard about that."

"Joe told me." She didn't bother to add that he should have. According to Joe, the glow-in-the-dark picture of Jesus and the children did what nothing else had. It allowed Sarah to go peacefully to sleep with just a night-light.

"I'm grateful it worked, okay? So what kind of celebration are you planning?"

"The idea is that we'll come down to the beach

this evening. We'll build a campfire, cook some hot-dogs and stay out until after dark. With our flash-lights, of course.''

He lifted an eyebrow. ''I didn't know you were a Girl Scout, too.''

''There's a lot you don't know about me.'' That sounded like an invitation. Maybe she'd better change the subject. ''Anyway, we'd like to have you join us. If you can make the time.''

He was already shaking his head. ''I've got to work until dark. And then I'm meeting the plumbing con-tractor. You two go ahead without me.''

''Daniel…'' While she was marshaling arguments, he was walking away. He'd swarmed up the ladder by the time she reached him. ''Daniel, please.''

His frown warned her off. *Private Property*, it seemed to say. ''I can't. Hey, I'll try to spend more time with Sarah, but this is too important to let slide.''

More important than your daughter? The words hovered on her tongue, but she held them back. She didn't want to alienate him so completely that he'd be too stubborn to admit he was wrong. Which he was. She spun and started for the house.

When she returned alone, Joe gave her a sympa-thetic look. ''Wouldn't stop?''

''No.'' She turned to Sarah. ''Ready for a rest?''

Sarah pouted.

''Remember, we decided you'd take a nap so you could stay up late for our picnic on the beach tonight. Remember?''

''Okay.'' Sarah gathered up the kitten. ''Okay.''

''Good.'' Leigh smiled. At least one of the Greg-orys was being agreeable.

Once Sarah and the kitten were settled on Sarah's

bed, Leigh returned to the kitchen. She'd brought her laptop computer, intending to get out a few more job application letters while Sarah slept.

Joe peered over her shoulder at the screen. "How's the search going?"

She shrugged. "Not bad. Lots of leads, but nothing too promising yet."

"Seems to me you could find a teaching job pretty easily."

He had to know, of course. Daniel would have told him. "I'm not in the market for a teaching position."

"Seems a shame, a good teacher like you."

Leigh's hands stilled on the keys, and his words echoed in her mind. "I used to think I was a good teacher. Now...I guess I'm not so sure."

Joe patted her shoulder. "'Course you are. Look what you've done with Sarah already. Wouldn't know she was the same child as when she came."

"She is making progress, isn't she?" She glanced up at him.

"Sure thing. Why, when that youngster first came here, I couldn't tell what she was like. All wrapped up in a prickly little ball, she was. Acting like a baby, most of the time."

She probably shouldn't ask, but she was going to. "Why do you think that was?"

"Guess maybe that's how her mama treated her. And that aunt of hers. Like she was a baby or a doll, instead of a real little girl."

"I take it you didn't like Ashley much." Okay, she shouldn't pump Joe for information. But she'd never get it from Daniel, and she just couldn't let go. She had to understand.

Joe shook his head. "Like? No, I guess I didn't.

Oh, she was a pretty thing. Beautiful, folks would say. But all she cared about was what was good for Ashley. She had to do what she wanted, no matter what.''

No matter what it did to Daniel or to Sarah, that was what he meant. Leigh reminded herself that this was Joe's view of things. He'd be on Daniel's side, and naturally he wouldn't think much of the wife who'd walked out on him. Still, there was a sad ring of truth in his words.

"You been thinking that Sarah belongs here, not away at some school, haven't you?" Joe said.

Leigh jerked up her head and met Joe's eyes in amazement. "What…how did you know that?"

"I've seen your face when Daniel talks about that school he's so determined to send Sarah to. You don't think that's for our little Sarah, do you?"

"I'm not sure." Leigh frowned. She probably shouldn't talk about this with Joe, but he loved Sarah. He seemed to be about the only thing close to a family that Daniel had. And maybe he could help. "I'm not sure what's best for Sarah."

"Seems to me a person could find out if Sarah could go to a regular school or not. Seems to me a person might try out that summer thing they do at the elementary school."

"How did you…" Well, of course Joe knew about the summer program. He knew everything that happened on the island. But to have Sarah try that program, even as a visitor… What if she wasn't ready? What if it turned into a disaster?

Are you sure you're not worried about how you would cope? a small voice asked in her mind. *If Sarah goes, you'd have to go, too. You'd be back in a school again.*

"Seems to me it might answer some questions," Joe said. "For both of you."

"I'm not sure Sarah's ready for that." *Or that I am, either.*

The door to the kitchen swung open, and Sarah stumbled in. "Sas-sy." Her lip trembled, and her eyes filled with tears. She brought her fingertips together, then spread them out and down. "Lost."

Daniel wrestled the two-by-four into place, then stopped, mopping his brow, and glared at the plank. He couldn't blame his foul temper on the piece of lumber, much as he'd like to. No, Leigh was the source, Leigh and her assumptions about what he should do.

Didn't she realize he was doing the best he could for his daughter? He didn't have to explain himself to her.

If that was true, why had he spent the last hour arguing with her in his mind, effectively showing her that he was right and she was wrong?

He glanced down at the water jug. The sun's angle hit it now, and drinking the water in it was about as appealing as drinking bathwater. "Hit" was the right word. The heat struck him like a blow each time he moved out of the shade.

Joe must be making a statement of his own today. Usually he brought down some lunch. Looked as if Joe had sided with Leigh in this ridiculous idea that he could take time from work to sit down at the lunch table.

Well, Joe was wrong, too. But since the old man had decided to be stubborn, it appeared he'd have to go up to the house for some food. And while he was there he'd give that obstinate old man a piece of his mind.

He'd gotten up the path almost to the toolshed, when a flash of something orange caught his eye. No, orange and white. What was that silly kitten doing outside without Sarah?

He started toward it, annoyed. The kitten looked up, gave him a wide-eyed stare, and then scurried through the crack beneath the door of the toolshed.

Stupid beast didn't know when it was well off. It could be curled up on a cushion in the kitchen, but instead it was wandering off, likely to get lost or to make a meal for a hungry critter. He'd better round it up before that happened, or Sarah would be heart-broken.

He opened the shed door slowly, ready to pounce on the kitten if it tried to run. Its yellow eyes glowed in the dark shed as it backed cautiously under the old workbench.

"Come here, you dumb animal." He held out his hand, snapping his fingers, forcing his tone to soften. "Come on, I'm not going to hurt you."

The kitten advanced slightly, sniffing. Another step and he'd have it. The kitten moved; he grabbed; the kitten darted back under the workbench. And behind him, faster than he could turn, the toolshed door swung closed with a creak and a final thud.

He groped his way through the sudden dark until he reached the door. He slid his hand down the rough wooden panel until he reached the handle, then yanked. Nothing. The door had latched itself, and he was trapped.

Muttering, he pounded on the door. "Hey! Leigh! Joe! Does anyone hear me?"

Nothing. The answering silence was infuriating. He pounded harder, yelling at the top of his lungs. Surely they could hear him in the kitchen, even if they had the door closed. Why didn't anyone come?

He yelled again, pounding until it seemed the blows echoed inside his head. Finally he stopped, breathing hard. Might as well stop acting like an idiot. No one could hear him. He'd just have to wait it out. Sooner or later, someone would notice he was gone. Or more likely notice the kitten was gone. Either way, someone would come looking.

His eyes had adjusted to the dim light that filtered under the door, and he spotted an old burlap feed bag. After spreading it on the dusty floor, he sat down and leaned against a barrel. When he got out of there, he was going to have a few words to say to Leigh about that kitten she'd let him in for.

As if it had heard his thoughts, the kitten padded across the floor and sniffed at his hand. He scratched the animal tentatively with one finger.

"Sassy, that's your name, isn't it? Well, Sassy, look at this fix you've gotten us into."

Locked in a dark shed when there was work to be done, talking to a cat. Great way to spend an afternoon.

The kitten nuzzled his hand, as if to remind him that he'd stopped petting it. He stroked the soft fur and got a resounding purr in response. It was like having a motor running under his hand.

"Okay, you're decent enough, for a cat. But I don't want to spend the day in here with you."

He nearly jumped up and pounded again, but that would be futile. Futile to shout and shout and not make anyone hear.

His hand slowed on the cat's fur. Was that what it was like for Sarah? Did she feel trapped, raging, unable to make other people understand her? Was that what hid behind her dark eyes?

The realization was a blow to his heart, like that moment in the doctor's office when he'd told them Sarah was deaf. Then it had just been words, words he'd kept trying to deny. Now... Maybe now he'd begun to understand, just a little, what it was like to be Sarah.

A distant sound reached his ears. Voices. Leigh and Joe, probably looking for the cat, not him. He stood up, tucking the kitten safely into the curve of his arm, and pounded on the door.

"Hey! In here! The toolshed!"

"What on earth...?" Leigh's voice came closer. "Daniel? Where are you?"

He gritted his teeth. "Locked in the toolshed. Open the door."

He was sure he heard a chuckle from Joe. Then the key turned in the lock and the door swung open.

Daniel blinked in the sudden light. Leigh, Joe and Sarah stood staring at him, wearing identical expressions of surprise.

"Daniel, what happened? What are you doing?"

Wordlessly, he held out the kitten.

"Sassy!" Sarah ran to him and scooped the kitten into her arms, snuggling it against her face. She'd probably been feeling about the way he had when she was lost, and his heart suddenly hurt at the thought.

He squatted in front of her, patting the kitten's soft fur. "It's okay, sweetie. The kitty's fine." He made an effort to sign. "She's fine."

"Thank goodness." Leigh reached over to ruffle

the kitten's fur. "We knew Sassy was missing. We didn't know you were or we'd have been looking."

He stood up slowly, eyes fixed on her face. She was blushing, just a little. Maybe she expected him to be angry with her about the wandering kitten.

"No problem," he said lightly. "I didn't expect anyone to send a search party out for me. Now, if I had four paws and purred…"

She smiled. "I promise we'd look for you. Even without the purring."

Joe touched Sarah's shoulder. "Come on, now, sugar. Let's give that kitten something to eat. Maybe that'll convince her not to go wandering." He led Sarah and the kitten toward the kitchen.

Daniel fell into step beside Leigh. Their arms brushed as they walked up the narrow path, and he felt the warmth that radiated from her. The light jasmine scent she wore teased his senses.

He shook his head. *Think about something else.*

"Funny thing being stuck in there, not able to make anyone hear. Really makes you angry. Frustrated. Like yelling or throwing something."

She looked at him, those sea-green eyes questioning, as if she probed beyond the surface of his words, searching for what lay beneath. "I guess it would feel that way."

"Sort of the way Sarah feels sometimes, maybe. When people don't understand."

Leigh nodded, her face grave. "Yes, I think that's exactly what it's like."

"So." He took a deep breath and forced himself to try to find the signs. "What time are we going on the picnic tonight?"

Chapter Nine

For a moment Leigh didn't get it. Then she realized what he meant, and happiness flooded through her. Daniel had changed his mind, had decided to put his daughter first, and she hadn't done a thing.

"You're coming on the picnic? That's wonderful, Daniel."

He shrugged, his eyes fixed on Sarah as she went up the steps ahead of them. "Getting over her fear of the dark is something to celebrate. Besides, I haven't had a toasted marshmallow in a long time. We are having marshmallows, aren't we?"

"Couldn't have a campfire without them." Leigh scribbled a mental note to run to the store. Eating toasted marshmallows was a small price to pay for the major stride Daniel seemed to have made in his understanding of Sarah.

Daniel lifted an eyebrow. "And hotdogs?"

"And hotdogs." She stopped on the stairs, looking up at him. "I knew that kitten was a good idea. I just didn't realize how good."

He smiled slowly, the fine sun lines at the corners of his dark eyes crinkling. "You think I needed to be locked in the shed all alone."

"I think…" Her throat had gone dry. "I think it didn't hurt you any."

He laughed and turned to open the door. She could breathe again.

Daniel had made progress. Maybe that suggestion of Joe's wasn't so impossible after all. Maybe, if she brought it up at the right time, in the right way, Daniel would be willing to listen with an open mind.

If she took Sarah to the summer program at Mark and Meggie's school… Her mind wanted to back away from that thought. If she did, Sarah wouldn't be the only one going into a difficult situation. The experience had just as much potential to wound Leigh as it did Sarah.

She bit her lip. She couldn't refuse to do something that might make all the difference for Sarah and Daniel just because it would hurt her. She'd find a chance to bring it up tonight.

Tonight, when they were alone on the beach. That insidious warmth rippled through her again. Daniel was coming. She'd gotten what she wanted. Now she had to figure out how to deal with it.

"Look at that," Daniel said. Leigh watched as he lifted Sarah in his arms, pointing out across silvery ripples of the outgoing tide. "See there? Dolphins."

Leigh's breath caught in her throat as the dolphins wheeled slowly, parallel to the beach. Their arching bodies gleamed in the fading light. "No matter how often I see them, I'm still stunned. They're so beautiful."

"And not really afraid of people." Daniel set Sarah down, and a wavelet rippled over her bare feet. "I'll take you out in the kayak sometime. You can really get close to them."

She nodded. Daniel said that so easily, as if a future existed in which the two of them would be doing things together.

Sarah splashed through the water, then stopped, squatting to inspect a shell left behind by the tide. Daniel bent down next to her, indicating something. His hand, broad and strong, touched Sarah's back with infinite tenderness, curving protectively.

Once again, Leigh's breath caught in her throat. This was just as beautiful as the wheeling of the dolphins, just as natural and elemental. She'd seen him hoist a two-by-four and wield a hammer as easily as some men might wield a pen. But he was capable of such enormous gentleness where his daughter was concerned.

Leigh shook her head. Daniel loved his child—that was all. And here she was, turning as soft at the sight as those marshmallows they intended to toast. She had to get a grip on her emotions. She couldn't let Daniel Gregory affect her this way.

Apparently finished with the shell, Daniel stood, glanced around and smiled. He held out his hand to Leigh.

"Come on, slowpoke. We have some serious beachcombing to do, remember?"

"I'm keeping up." Her voice sounded the slightest bit breathless as she put her hand in his. "You two are the ones who keep stopping to look at things." She shook her head. "I don't understand it. You spot things I don't even see."

He shrugged. "All a matter of what you're used to looking for. I've been around the ocean my entire life. Guess I just see things automatically."

"Did you grow up on the island?"

"Here? No." Daniel frowned. For a moment she thought he'd put on his Keep Out expression, but then he went on. "I grew up in a little tidewater town north of here, on an island so small you've never heard of it. My daddy was a fisherman. When he was sober."

The edge of bitterness startled her. "I'm sorry. I didn't mean to bring up something you'd rather not talk about."

Their hands, still linked, swung between them for three steps, four. "No secret, I guess. I was the eldest. Four younger ones. Long as I could remember, Mama was just...defeated."

A lot of pain dwelled behind the soft-spoken words; Leigh could feel it. She could also read between the lines. "So you tried to parent the others."

"Guess I did." His eyes were on Sarah. "Must not have done that great a job. They're scattered now. I don't hear from them from one year to the next."

"And your parents?"

"Both dead." His voice didn't change, but his fingers tightened, probably involuntarily, on hers.

Pain and guilt. Maybe her own experience made it easy for her to recognize them. Her heart hurt at the thought of the serious, responsible little boy who'd undoubtedly given up his childhood trying to raise his siblings.

"You were just a child. You can't blame yourself for someone else's failings."

"Maybe not. But I surely can blame myself if I don't do everything I can for Sarah."

That might be an opportunity to talk about what really was good for Sarah, but she couldn't take it. Daniel had just opened up to her in a way she'd never thought he would. In the wake of what he'd just told her, how could she say anything he might interpret as a criticism of his parenting?

Sarah stopped, pointing down at something in the sand, and the opportunity, if it had existed, was gone. Daniel let go of Leigh's hand to splash over to her. Leigh came up to them just as he dug something carefully out of the sand.

"Look, Sarah." He rinsed it off in a wavelet and held it out to his daughter. "Look at the shell."

Sarah took the shell in both hands, her tiny face awestruck. The shell had a rough, weathered exterior, but the inside was an iridescent, pearl-like pink, smooth as satin.

"Oh, Sarah, it's beautiful." Leigh knelt next to her, glancing up at Daniel. "What is it?"

"Whelk." Daniel ran his finger over the rounded peaks on the end of the shell. "Knobbed whelk, to be exact. Sort of like the conch shells they find in the Caribbean."

"Lovely." She clasped Sarah's fingers around it. "You can keep it on your shelf."

Sarah caressed the shell for a moment, then she shook her head. Smiling, she held it out to Leigh.

Daniel grinned, ruffling his daughter's hair. "Looks like Sarah knows just what she wants to do with her prize."

"Sarah, honey." Leigh stroked the child's cheek. "Are you sure? Don't you want to keep it?"

Sarah shook her head again and patted Leigh's hand. "Yours," she said.

Leigh felt tears welling. "Thank you." She held out her arms for a hug, and Sarah walked into them. "Thank you, Sarah."

Little arms around her neck, a soft cheek pressed against hers. She'd told herself she wouldn't get emotionally involved this time...promised herself she wouldn't open her heart. She'd just been kidding herself; she knew that now.

For better or worse, it was too late. She already loved Sarah. Whatever happened, she had to help her. And no matter what the cost, that meant making Daniel realize he was wrong about sending her away to school.

Daniel rotated the stick slowly, watching the hotdog start to bubble. He wanted it to be perfect. He glanced at Leigh and Sarah, firelight reflected from their faces. He wanted everything about this night to be perfect.

Leigh pulled a roll from the basket Joe had provided. "What does Sarah like on her hotdog?"

"Mustard. Just like her daddy."

"You've got it." She held out the roll, and he slid the hotdog onto it from the stick. "Here you are, Sarah." She squirted the mustard onto it. "One perfect hotdog."

Sarah took it carefully, bit into it and smiled. She looked at him, mustard decorating her face, and his heart turned over. His little Sarah, relaxed, slightly dirty, happy... It was more than he'd dared hope for when she came to live with him. He owed it all to a chance encounter on the beach.

"How about you?" Leigh asked. "Aren't you having one?'' She fit a hotdog on the stick he'd cut for her and held it over the fire.

"One?" He lifted his eyebrows, reaching for the package. "I might just have two or three."

"Better save room for the marshmallows you wanted. I got the large bag."

"Don't you worry about that. What I don't eat I'll bet Sarah will."

Sarah grinned at him, as if she understood, then suddenly frowned and slapped at her arm.

"Ouch." Leigh rubbed her own arm. "Maybe being out here at night wasn't just a great idea."

"Attack of the no-see-ums." Daniel grinned, reaching for the repellent he'd tucked into the basket. "I have just the thing. Come here, Sarah."

Sarah put her hotdog on a paper plate and scampered to him, holding out her arms. He smoothed the repellent down them quickly.

"Here you go. This will keep the bugs away."

She wrinkled up her nose, and Leigh laughed. "Sarah doesn't like the smell, but it doesn't bother me. I'll put up with anything, as long as it keeps the bugs from biting."

He dabbed some on Sarah's ankles, then reached across, his hand still oily, and ran it down Leigh's arm.

Her laughter stilled suddenly. His eyes met hers. Hers were startled, a little wary, widening with the same recognition that had to be mirrored in his.

"Better get some on your neck, too." His voice sounded rough to his ears. "The more tender the skin, the better, as far as they're concerned." His hand moved toward the smooth column of her neck.

Quickly she took the bottle from him. "I can get it."

That was probably better. Safer, at any rate, if not necessarily better. He watched her smooth the lotion along her skin, and his palm tingled as if his were the hand that did it.

Whoa, back up. What had happened to his resolution where Leigh was concerned? Well, he had to cool it. No matter how impossible it seemed, he had to control what he did, and he had to start right now.

"Better?" he asked as Leigh capped the bottle.

Leigh sniffed at her arm. "I probably smell pretty awful, but as long as the bugs think so, too, that's all right."

He grinned. "We'll all smell like wood smoke before too long, anyway." He looked at Sarah and gestured. "Another hotdog, sugar?"

Sarah shook her head, eyeing the bag of marshmallows.

A half-dozen toasted marshmallows later, Sarah seemed satisfied. She leaned against Leigh, eyes half-closed, staring into the fire.

Outside the circle of firelight, the darkness pressed around them. The murmur of the waves was soft now at low tide. A cry pierced the darkness, and he felt Leigh wince in surprise.

"Just an owl." He gestured. "Hunting in the dunes."

She shivered, moving a little closer to him. "Sounds eerie."

"The beach is different at night. Lots of creatures come out that the sunbathers never see."

She tilted back her head. "You never see stars like that anywhere else, do you?"

He studied the silken line of her neck. Then, reluctantly, he followed the direction of her gaze. "Not in the city, that's for sure." The canopy of the heavens spread from horizon to horizon.

"'When I look at the heavens, the work of Thy fingers, the moon and the stars, which Thou hast established...'" Her voice was soft. "One of my favorite verses."

"How do you sign *star*?"

She showed him, and he mimicked her movement. Sarah, snuggled against Leigh, didn't pay attention.

"I guess maybe lessons are over for tonight."

Leigh nodded, stroking Sarah's hair. "I think she's accomplished enough for one day."

Watching her with his child—her tenderness, her warmth—did things to him he didn't expect. Made him almost wish he could still believe in love and trust and happy endings.

"This is a first," he said lightly, because he didn't trust himself to say anything serious. "Sarah's first hotdog roast, first campfire."

Leigh's gaze met his over his child's head. "You don't think her mother did anything like this with her?"

He poked at the fire. "Ashley never liked outdoor things. I don't suppose that changed after she left here."

"Weren't you..." Leigh's voice was soft, hesitant. "Well, it doesn't sound as if the two of you were very well suited to each other."

"You might say that." He poked the fire again, and a cluster of sparks flew upward, dancing against the blackness, echoing the starry expanse above them. "In fact, that's probably the understatement of a lifetime. Haven't you ever noticed how often people pick the person who's exactly wrong for them?''

She frowned. Maybe that didn't happen in her world. Maybe Leigh didn't make mistakes like that.

''I guess so,'' she said slowly. ''At least, well, I've dated people who were wrong for me. But usually I figured it out pretty quickly. Once I got so far as to bring one of them home.'' Her smile flickered. ''My parents were polite, but Jamie's comments about him made me mad. They also made me think.''

''You were lucky.'' He didn't want to drift back to the subject of his marriage. Didn't want to try to explain to Leigh how he could have made a fundamental mistake about something that had seemed the most important thing in his life. ''So, what about all these boyfriends? Anybody serious?''

She took her turn to poke at the fire. ''No, not for a while. Actually, maybe none of them was serious. I just thought so at the time.''

''No one?''

She shrugged. ''I guess it's the old story. I never found the right one. I wanted...'' Her voice trailed off.

Somehow he needed to hear what the rest of that sentence would be. ''Wanted what, Leigh?''

She smiled down at Sarah, asleep now with her head pillowed on Leigh's leg. ''What Jamie has, I guess. Something that would last a lifetime. Forever. Children. When I make those promises...'' She stopped, and he saw the blood come up under that creamy skin.

''You'll take them seriously.'' He frowned. ''I thought I did. Maybe I was wrong. Or maybe Ashley was.'' He'd gotten right back onto the subject he'd thought to avoid. "Or maybe what we had together wasn't strong enough to withstand trouble." He scooped up a handful of sand and let it drift through his fingers. "Isn't there something in the Bible about that? Building your house on the sand? Maybe that's what we did."

Leigh's hand covered his. "I'm sorry. I didn't mean to bring up something painful."

"You didn't. I did." Her face, reflecting the fire light, seemed to draw his hand irresistibly. "There's something about you, Leigh. I tell you things I haven't talked about to another soul."

His fingers brushed the curve of her cheek, and her skin was smooth and satiny as the inside of the shell they'd found. *Danger,* a little voice said inside him, but he ignored it. He ran his finger along the line of her jaw, tilting her face up toward his.

Her skin flushed; her eyes darkened. She put one hand on his arm. To push him away? No, to draw him closer.

"Leigh." His voice was a whisper.

Her lips parted. Maybe she was going to say something, but his mouth closed on hers before she could speak.

She tasted so sweet, so very sweet. He drew her a little closer. Her hand touched his face, butterfly light, caressing the skin.

He dragged his mouth from hers, pulse pounding in his temples. *Slow down. Take it easy.* He kissed that misplaced dimple next to her mouth, then found her lips again.

Sarah stirred. Leigh drew back, her green eyes huge. He had to tear his gaze from her soft lips. He shrugged, a little ruefully.

"I wasn't going to do that. But if you expect me to be sorry, you'll have a long wait."

A smile trembled on her lips. "No." The word was breathless. "I'm not sorry, either." She looked down at Sarah. "But I think maybe it's time to call it a night."

He let his hand drift lightly across her cheek one more time, tucked a strand of hair behind her ear. "I think you're right."

Leigh packed up the picnic basket, wondering why her hands weren't shaking. She certainly felt as if everything inside her shook. As if her whole world had moved slightly on its axis.

It was a kiss; that was all. Well, several kisses. It didn't necessarily have to mean anything, except that Daniel was attracted to her. Not anything at all.

So why couldn't she prevent the smile that curved her lips or the singing that seemed to be taking place inside her head?

"Tired, sugar?" Daniel helped Sarah to her feet. "Time to go in."

"You carry her," Leigh said quickly. "I can manage the rest of the stuff." She scooped up basket and blanket, then switched on her flashlight.

"I'll carry the blanket, too, at least." He took it from her, his fingers lingering for a moment on her arm. Then he turned to pick up Sarah. "Off we go."

Leigh thought he'd move up the path ahead of her. Instead he tossed the blanket over his shoulder. His fingers encircled her wrist, helping her focus the flashlight. She could feel her pulse beating against his palm.

Was this a mistake? She didn't know. She knew

only that she was happier than she'd been in a very long time. Surely something that brought this much happiness couldn't be wrong.

With trees screening the moon, the path was black. Daniel's hand, steady on her wrist, led her along the small beam of the flashlight. It showed them just enough of the path for them to keep on walking.

They reached the house and started up the steps, into the circle of light from the porch. Daniel smiled down at her as he opened the door, and his eyes seemed filled with promise.

He stepped into the hall and stopped dead. Leigh stopped, too, and her breath caught in her throat.

A woman stood in the living-room doorway, hands out to the frame on either side. Dark red hair curled around her face, spilled to her shoulders. Leigh felt the hallway spin around her.

Chapter Ten

❧

Of course it wasn't Ashley. The world righted. The resemblance to the photograph was just that, a resemblance.

Sarah slid from Daniel's arms and ran toward the woman. Leigh heard him take a breath.

"Judith. You're here." He didn't sound particularly pleased to see her.

So this was Judith, his wife's sister...the woman who apparently had taken on much of Sarah's care. The woman who hadn't wanted to expose Sarah to other children.

Leigh discovered she was tensing and forced herself to take a deep breath. She shouldn't make assumptions about the woman based on a few casual comments. That wasn't fair.

"Sweet baby." Judith lifted Sarah in her arms, kissing her, patting her. "My sweet baby, I've missed you so much."

Daniel put down the things he'd carried, then took the basket from Leigh and set it on the hall table. His expression had tightened, and a small muscle twitched beside his lips. Leigh found herself studying the firm line of his mouth, remembering... She yanked her mind away from that thought.

"You've taken us by surprise." Daniel's voice sounded carefully neutral. "Why didn't you let me know you were coming?"

"I didn't want you to fuss. I know how busy you are right now."

Judith's gaze went from Daniel to Leigh, bright and inquisitive, and Leigh found herself stiffening again.

"I'd still have liked to know to expect you. Joe could have gotten a room ready."

Daniel crossed to her, hesitated, then dropped a light kiss on her cheek. It seemed to Leigh that neither of them enjoyed it much.

"Oh, I've taken care of all that." Judith turned, still holding Sarah cradled in her arms like a baby. She walked into the living room and sat down, snuggling Sarah against her. "I've made up a bed in the room I used when I came before. I'm not going to be any trouble to you at all. I just had to see my darling baby."

So Judith planned to stay in the house. Well, of course she would. She was family, after all, and Daniel's guest rooms weren't occupied. Leigh suppressed a stab of... What? Jealousy? Apprehension?

Leigh hovered in the living-room doorway, not sure what she should do. Why hadn't Daniel bothered to introduce her? Had she gone invisible all of a sudden?

As if he read her mind, Daniel touched her shoulder lightly. "Judith, I'd like you to meet Leigh Christopher. She's taking care of Sarah now."

"I see."

Judith's eyebrows lifted, her eyes assessing, and Leigh had a sudden image of what the woman must have seen when the three of them came through the door: Daniel's hand clasping hers.

"It's nice to meet you, Leigh."

Leigh murmured an appropriate response, wondering just how much Judith meant that. She turned to Daniel. "Would you like me to get Sarah ready for bed, so you and your guest can visit?"

"Certainly not." Judith spoke before Daniel could answer. "I've been looking forward to putting Sarah to bed myself. You wouldn't want to take that pleasure away from me, would you?"

There wasn't much Leigh could say to that. "Of course not, if you're sure."

"I am." Judith stroked Sarah's hair. "Daniel, what on earth have you done? What happened to Sarah's hair?"

Daniel frowned. "I had it cut. It's a lot more practical, and Sarah loves it."

Again Judith's gaze shifted from Daniel to Leigh, and Leigh had the feeling she was making judgments. Then Judith got up, still holding Sarah.

"Much as I'd like to chat with Leigh, I'm sure she's ready to go home."

That seemed clear enough. She was definitely not welcome at this family reunion. She looked at Daniel, but he watched Judith. The connection between her and Daniel when they'd come up from the beach, the promise she'd seen in his eyes—they had vanished like fog in the sunlight.

"I'll be on my way, then. See you tomorrow."

"I'll walk you out." Daniel turned quickly to follow her.

They stopped on the porch, standing in the yellow glow of its light. Daniel rested his fist against a column and let out his breath in an exasperated sigh. "Sorry about that. I'm afraid Judith tends to take over where Sarah is concerned."

"It's okay." Leigh hovered on the top step, inches from him. She could only hope it really was okay, that Judith's arrival wouldn't change everything.

"Look, I'll see you in the morning." His gaze lingered on her face, and the night sounds pressed around them. "Thanks for the picnic. For everything."

This was not the moment to bring up her thoughts about involving Sarah in a regular school. Not with what was obviously a very opinionated extra person around. "Good night, Daniel."

He nodded, his mind clearly on something else. "Good night, Leigh."

Leigh got in the car and watched the door close behind Daniel. It shut her out. She started the car.

Be rational, some part of her mind urged. She couldn't expect that momentary closeness with Daniel to survive in the face of a visit from his sister-in-law.

And just what else might Judith's visit upset? The little she'd heard about Judith's attitude toward Sarah filled her with apprehension.

A pair of deer appeared suddenly in her headlights and Leigh stopped, clutching the wheel, until they'd crossed the narrow road and plunged into the pines.

One thing was certain. Leigh stepped on the accelerator. Judith couldn't be allowed to interfere with Sarah's progress. Leigh would be tactful, polite and professional, but she'd keep that from happening...somehow.

* * *

When she got to the house the next morning, Daniel wasn't there. Telling herself she hadn't come to see him, Leigh went up to Sarah's room.

"There now, baby. We'll have you dressed in just a minute."

Leigh heard Judith before she reached the room. With a sense of foreboding, she paused in the doorway.

Sarah sat on the bed, passively letting her aunt put her arms into the sleeves of her shirt. Leigh clenched her teeth, counted to ten and reminded herself that she couldn't start a battle with Sarah's aunt. Or, at least, she shouldn't.

"Good morning." She smiled, signing to Sarah. "Did you sleep well?"

Sarah nodded, not signing back. She extended her foot and Judith put on her sock.

In the morning light, Judith's resemblance to the photo of her sister faded, almost disappearing. She had a stronger face than Ashley's, with broad cheekbones and fine lines around eyes and mouth. She finished dressing Sarah, then turned to Leigh, straightening her shoulders as if preparing for battle.

"You know, there's really no need for you to stay today. Sarah doesn't need a baby-sitter when I'm here."

Leigh hadn't expected quite so forceful an attack, and she stiffened. Was that what Daniel had said she was—a baby-sitter? Or was that Judith's interpretation of the situation? That, at least, she could clear up.

"I'm afraid there's been a misunderstanding. I'm not Sarah's sitter. I'm her teacher. Didn't Daniel explain that?"

Judith picked up the brush and began brushing Sarah's hair. "He did say something about that." She glanced at Leigh, the look challenging. "But surely that doesn't mean Sarah can't have a day off to visit with me."

"Of course you want to visit." Leigh's conscience stung her. Judith loved Sarah and wanted to spend time with her. The fact that Leigh didn't approve of Judith's methods of expressing that love really didn't matter.

"Tell you what." Maybe there was a compromise that would suit both of them. "Why don't you join us in our activities today. I'm sure Sarah would like that."

Judith looked as if she'd like to argue, but then she shrugged. "Of course. Let's do that."

That might, Leigh decided by the afternoon, have been the worst suggestion she'd ever made. Judith participated, all right. Unfortunately her method of participating was to do everything for Sarah.

When they painted, she guided the brush in Sarah's hand, clucking over every spilled drop. When Leigh got out the flash cards, she insisted Sarah wasn't old enough to understand them. When Leigh suggested a trip to the beach, Judith countered that it was too hot and Sarah really needed a nap.

Worst of all was the effect Judith had on Sarah. In Judith's presence, Sarah suddenly became a baby again, passively allowing her aunt to do everything. She didn't try to talk, didn't assert herself, didn't even want to play with her kitten. Instead, she returned to the doll and the cradle, repeating her motions over and over under Judith's doting supervision.

Leigh finally sought out Joe. She found him in the kitchen.

"How long is she staying?" She knew Joe would understand exactly whom she was talking about.

He shrugged, frowning down at the pastry he was rolling out. "Don't know. Nobody tells me anything."

"That's because you always know it without being told." Leigh leaned against the counter next to him and snitched a sliver of dough. "Come on, what's your best guess?"

"She brought an awful lot of clothes," Joe said mournfully. "Reckon she doesn't plan on going home any time soon."

"That's...not good." The dough turned to ashes in her mouth. "I mean, I realize she's Sarah's aunt. She loves her."

Joe brought his rolling pin down with a thump. "Maybe. But she's not good for her." He looked at Leigh. "Somebody ought to do something."

"Like what?" Leigh suspected she was the somebody he had in mind.

Joe shrugged. "Daniel's down to the marina, getting the boat ready to take out. Seems to me if somebody went down there, it'd be a good spot for a private talk."

"You're a conniver, you know that?" Leigh smiled at him.

He grinned back. "I'm right, sure as the sun shines."

He probably was at that. "Will you keep an eye on things here?"

"Sure will."

All right. She'd go to the marina and have that

private conversation with Daniel. She'd explain her concerns about the effect Judith had on Sarah.

Leigh ignored the queasiness in her stomach. She'd even talk to him about letting Sarah participate in the program at Mark and Meggie's school. She could win him over; she knew she could. She just had to convince him that it was best for Sarah.

She kept telling herself that during the drive to the marina on Skull Creek, the tidal creek that cut the island nearly in half. Josh kept his boat at the same marina, so she knew just where to go.

At this hour of the day, most of the fishing boats were out. She walked along the dock, glancing at the slips, until she saw movement on one of the boats. Daniel.

"Hey."

He looked up, shading his eyes from the sun. "Leigh." His eyes widened with alarm. "Is something wrong?"

"No, not at all." She should have realized he'd jump to that conclusion over her unexpected visit. "Sarah's fine. I just wanted to talk with you, and Joe told me you were here."

Daniel nodded, his face relaxing. "Got two fishermen coming to stay in a couple of days, so I had to get the boat ready." He held out his hand. "Come aboard. I'm almost done."

Her hand clasped firmly in his, she clambered into the boat, trying to ignore the effect his nearness had on her. She glanced around. "Similar to Josh's boat, isn't it?"

"His is a little bigger." Daniel rested a possessive hand on the rail, stroking the craft as if it were alive.

"This is a twenty-one footer. All I need for the size parties I take out, and small enough to handle on my own." He gestured to the swivel chair behind the controls. "Have a seat while I finish stowing this gear, and then we can talk."

She watched him move efficiently about the boat, quick and competent. Everything on the *Dolphin* was tidy, clean, shining. Josh claimed you could tell a lot about a man by how he kept his boat. By that measure, Daniel scored high.

"Okay, done." Daniel looked at her, and his eyes seemed to warm. "Tell you what. If you're not in a hurry, let's take her out a ways. I want to be sure everything's running smoothly."

She lifted an eyebrow. "It almost sounds like you're making excuses."

"Okay, I'm not too eager to get back to the house." He grinned. "Judith never has approved of me, and it shows. Gets under my skin sometimes."

She probably shouldn't play hooky like this. But she was going to. "Sounds great. I'll get the lines."

Daniel pulled on a T-shirt, then took her place at the console. She could feel him watching her as she unfastened the lines.

"Josh been giving you seamanship lessons?"

She smiled. "Mark and Meggie. It's mortifying to discover that small children know more than you do."

"They've been on boats all their lives." He eased the *Dolphin* away from the dock. "Guess maybe I should be taking Sarah out. I hadn't thought of it."

"That's a good idea."

She came back to stand next to him. They moved into the creek, and the boat took on life as it caught the tide, bucking over the waves. She braced her hand on the edge of the console. The breeze ruffled her hair and salt air filled her lungs.

"Great day." Daniel waved to an incoming craft as they putted slowly down the No Wake zone.

"Great feeling." She took another breath. "It's like being...free."

He nodded, glancing at a brown pelican diving for a fish. "Free. That's a good way to put it. When I'm out on the boat, I feel as if I don't have to think about anything else."

And her whole purpose in being here was to force him to confront something he'd rather not face. But she didn't have to do it right now. She could just enjoy this for a moment or two longer.

Daniel swung the boat in a wide arc into the channel that led to the ocean. The movement threw her into him, pressing her against the smooth, hard muscles of his arm and shoulder.

Warmth closed around her. She wanted to put both arms around him, feel the combination of sun and wind and Daniel.

She steadied herself and pulled away. Daniel reached out with the hand that didn't hold the wheel and drew her close to his side again.

"Lady, you drive me crazy." His voice was a murmur under the sound of the engine.

"I think...the feeling's mutual." She let her hand rest on his shoulder. "But maybe it's not such a good idea."

He must have heard the doubt in her voice. "I know." He let out his breath in an exasperated sigh and released her. "Okay, I'll play tour guide, if that's what you want." He gestured toward the salt marsh on their left. "Over there you see a blue heron shopping for supper."

Leigh's throat tightened in frustration. Why couldn't this be simple? Why couldn't they just be two people who were attracted to each other?

Because it isn't, the voice inside her head reminded her. *It isn't.* She'd be leaving the island, leaving him and Sarah, by the end of the summer. Her beliefs didn't include a casual affair, no matter how strong her feelings were.

And they were strong, way too strong. She'd never met a man who could engender that deep stab of longing Daniel did with just a glance from his dark eyes. But that just made it all the more dangerous.

Besides, there was Sarah, and her own conviction that Daniel's plans for his daughter were wrong. She couldn't muddy what she hoped to accomplish for Sarah by getting involved with the child's father.

Leigh cleared her throat. "Maybe we ought to get to what I wanted to talk to you about."

"Let me guess." Lines formed between his brows. "It's about Judith."

"In part. How long is she going to stay?"

Daniel's jaw clenched. "I don't know. If you'll recall, I didn't even invite her. But she's Sarah's aunt." He shot her a look that was half annoyance, half pleading. "I can't just ask her to leave."

"I understand." Leigh put her hand lightly on his shoulder again. "I know it's difficult. I'm just concerned about the effect she has on Sarah. It's as if Sarah turns into a baby again when she's around."

"That's how Judith's always treated her." His frown deepened, and that tiny muscle next to his mouth twitched. "I don't think she's ever realized what Sarah is capable of. As I didn't, until you."

The sudden intensity of his look brought the blood to her cheeks.

"I..." If he kept looking at her that way, she wouldn't be able to talk at all. She took a deep breath. "I'm just worried that it will put Sarah back if it goes on too long."

His fingers drummed lightly against the console. "Look, why don't we give it a day or two. Maybe when Judith sees you work with Sarah, she'll start to understand. It can't be easy for her to admit she's wrong. She's been the one to teach Sarah up to now."

He was probably being overly optimistic about the chance of Judith changing, but what else could she do? She couldn't expect him to cut Judith off.

"Why did Judith—" She stopped. Once more she was veering into personal territory.

They'd nearly reached the mouth of the creek. Beyond them, the ocean spread in a silvery expanse. Daniel concentrated as he turned the boat, making a wide, frothy arc across the surface on the water.

When they were headed back up the creek again, he stared straight ahead, eyes narrowed against the sun. "Ashley never really had the patience to try to teach Sarah anything." His voice was flat, as it often was when he spoke of Ashley. "Don't get me wrong—she loved her. She just couldn't find the time or the patience to spend on her."

Wasn't that what love was? Leigh tried to suppress the thought. She couldn't criticize someone she'd never met. She didn't understand what drove Ashley, and she didn't have the right to judge her. But she bled for Sarah.

"I'm sorry." That seemed a feeble response.

Daniel shook his head, as if shaking off sorrow. "Look, I promise that if Judith doesn't come around...or leave...in a couple of days, I'll talk to her."

She could sense the reluctance in him. Like most men, probably the last thing in the world he could stomach was a scene.

"You wouldn't be afraid of her reaction, would you?" she asked lightly.

"Guilty as charged." He grinned. "I'm a coward where that woman is concerned."

"At least you admit it."

The boat bucked over the wake of a larger fishing boat, and she grabbed Daniel's shoulder to steady herself. A mistake, she realized, when a breathless warmth blossomed inside her.

Daniel put his arm around her, steadying her. Then, slowly, he drew her closer. Sunlight, water, the salt tang of the sea, the warmth and strength of Daniel—they overpowered her senses.

Sarah. The school plan. She had to keep her mind on the reason she'd come here today.

Daniel looked at her, apparently sensing the things she didn't say.

"What?"

She shook her head. "You're reading my mind."

"You have a very transparent face. And honest eyes." His arm tightened around her, just a little. "Not made for keeping secrets."

"There was something else I wanted to talk to you about."

He sighed. "This isn't another kitten, is it?"

"No more kittens. It does have to do with Mark and Meggie, though, in a way."

He lifted an eyebrow. "Are you going to get to the point sometime today?"

"Mark and Meggie go to a half-day enrichment program at the elementary school right now." Was she doing this in the right way?

"And?"

He wasn't going to let her move slowly.

"And I think it might be a good idea to let Sarah visit the school a time or two. Take part in the program. She could—"

She suddenly became aware that he was no longer holding her. Both hands gripped the wheel, and his jaw had tightened.

"Daniel, this is something Sarah can do. Honestly. It would be good for her. And if she can function in a regular school with some extra help, then she wouldn't have to go away to school."

There, it was all out. All that she'd been thinking about Sarah. Probably not the most professional way of bringing it up, but being professional was a lost cause where Daniel and Sarah were concerned.

For a long moment Daniel didn't say anything. Then he turned to look at her, his face shuttered and frowning.

Leigh's heart sank. He wasn't going to listen to her.

Chapter Eleven

The "No" hovered on Daniel's lips, but something kept him from blurting it out. He'd given Leigh that instantaneous *no* several times, and each time she'd turned out to be right.

Not this time; he was sure of it. But he owed her more than a fast refusal.

They entered the Low Wake zone and he slowed. The sudden quiet made talking easier. The trouble lay in finding the right words to say.

Leigh watched him, concern darkening her eyes. She obviously expected an argument.

He blew out a breath in a frustrated sigh. "How can I make you understand?" *And agree,* a little voice added in his mind. That was really what he wanted, for Leigh to understand and to agree that the course he'd set for his daughter was the right one.

Leigh smiled, her face relaxing as she apparently realized he wasn't going to blow up at her. "Just tell me *yes*. I'll understand that."

"Leigh." He frowned down at his hands on the

wheel, trying to find the right words, the words that would convince her. "I realize you know a lot about educating deaf children."

"That's what those pieces of paper on my wall say." Leigh's voice was light but her eyes guarded.

"Look, I'm not crazy about Judith, but she knows Sarah as well as anyone." Guilt stabbed him. "She's been around her more than I have. And she's convinced that Sarah can't possibly get along in a regular school."

"I'm sure Judith's done a great deal for Sarah."

He sensed Leigh was picking her words carefully.

"But sometimes when you're very close to a child, you don't notice the way that child is growing. Changing."

Sarah had changed; he couldn't deny that. Changed since Leigh had entered her life. Their lives. But how could he believe that was enough?

"It's not just Judith. Ashley took Sarah for some kind of evaluation last year by a specialist. He's the one who recommended this school. He ought to know."

If he thought Leigh would bow to the opinion of Ashley's expert, he'd be wrong; he could tell. He could feel the resistance in her, feel the way she held back against his arguments.

When had he learned to read her so well? When had she become so familiar to him that he could understand and interpret every expression in those green eyes?

"He might be the best-known authority in the country, but it would still just be one person's opinion." Leigh's jaw tightened stubbornly. "Besides, we don't know how Ashley framed the question about

school. Did she even ask if he felt Sarah could function in a regular school with an interpreter?"

Leigh was coming up with questions he hadn't
thought to ask. "I don't know. But she said..." He
stopped, remembering what Ashley had said. Remembering the look in her eyes and the way it had made
him feel.

"What?" Leigh's voice gentled. She touched his
wrist lightly. "What did she say, Daniel?"

He concentrated on bringing the boat into the slip.
When it was docked to his satisfaction, he looked at
Leigh. The question was still there, in her eyes. The
question he didn't want to answer.

"She pointed out that I hadn't fulfilled my promises to her." He made his voice dry, as if it didn't
matter. As if it didn't still cut. "She said I owed it to
Sarah not to fail her."

Leigh's hand closed over his. He could feel her
caring through his skin, read it in her eyes.

"You haven't failed Sarah. You're a wonderful father." Tears suddenly sparkled in her eyes. "Honestly, Daniel. When I watch the two of you together,
I see so much love and trust there. That's not failure.
That's success."

A lump the size of an anchor lodged in his throat.
He swallowed hard. "That's why I have to do the
right thing. Sarah doesn't have anyone but me."

"I know. I'm not asking you to make any big decisions right now, Daniel. I just want you to let me
look into the possibility of having Sarah visit at Mark
and Meggie's school. That's all I want right now, just
to look into it. Then we'll talk."

A tear lingered on Leigh's cheek, and he reached
out to blot it away with one finger. How could he

argue with someone who cared that much about his child? He hadn't convinced her. Maybe he never could.

"All right, Leigh. You look into it. Then we'll talk."

The island had to be the wettest place in the world when it rained, Leigh decided. She drew into the school parking lot in a pelting downpour. The last few days had been filled with frustration as Sarah went steadily backward under Judith's constant babying. And Daniel had been unwilling, or maybe unable, to intervene.

She'd lost the ability to blame him for that after what he'd told her the day on the boat. Daniel hurt so much. He carried such a burden for the disintegration of his marriage. That pain had pushed him into making decisions for Sarah that Leigh was convinced were wrong.

But how could she argue, knowing what lay behind them? And Judith's presence had made the whole situation worse, much worse.

At least the end of that was in sight. Judith's vacation would be over in a few more days. She'd go back north, and Leigh would try to make up lost ground with Sarah.

Leigh cut the windshield wipers. Water flooded the windshield, obscuring her view of everything beyond it. She might as well have been in a submarine in the depths of the ocean.

After grabbing her umbrella, she ducked out into the downpour. The tropical storm that had been churning its way north from the Caribbean supposedly wasn't going to touch the island. But the rainfall on its fringes seemed to Leigh, unused to it, of biblical proportions.

All around her the rain intensified the verdant green of the island, turning it warm and steaming. The palmettos waved and danced along the crushed-shell path to the school, sending a deluge of water down her neck when the umbrella got away from her for a second.

Gasping with the shock, she darted under the veranda roof and yanked open the door, spilling into the hallway in a flurry of rain and palmetto fronds. She shook out her umbrella and took a deep breath.

School on a wet day... How could she possibly mistake the smell? If she were set down blindfolded in a school anywhere from Afghanistan to Zanzibar, she'd recognize it by the combination of aromas: wet slickers, wet sneakers, wet children. The scent clutched her heart like a vise.

Leigh propped her sopping umbrella in the stand. She would not think about what it meant to be in a school again. She would not remember, or compare, or open her heart to the pain of not belonging here.

Then a crocodile of children wound its way from room to room, and in an instant she was transported back to her school. Rain turned Philadelphia a shimmering silver gray, not a verdant green, but the feeling was the same. She might have been walking down those halls, hearing the children's shrill voices, watching the animated faces.

Except that there she'd have been surrounded by now, swept away in a current of children who knew her. Here she was the stranger, to be eyed curiously but not approached.

Struggling to suppress a sigh, she went to find the

office and check in. She'd do her observing; she'd try to set things up for Sarah. She'd try her hardest not to get involved.

A few minutes later Leigh paused outside the kindergarten classroom, took a deep breath and opened the door. Meggie, who must have been watching, saw her immediately and came running, paint-daubed hands outstretched.

The teacher, laughing, caught Meggie by her painting shirt. "Slow down, Meggie."

"But Ms. Carter, it's my auntie Leigh."

The woman's gaze met Leigh's over Meggie's head, and her eyes invited a shared laugh. "I figured that out, Meggie. But your aunt probably doesn't want to have paint all over her."

"Oh." Meggie looked at her hands, then divided a smile between Leigh and her teacher. "I forgot. We're painting, Aunt Leigh."

"So I see."

Cardboard furniture boxes, each set on an apron of newspaper, were being transformed by a coat of paint, enthusiastically if inexpertly applied.

"We're creating a colonial village."

Ms. Carter supplied the information before Leigh had to ask and admit she couldn't tell what it was.

"Each 'family' has its own house. Today we're painting them." She gave Meggie a little nudge. "You get back to your group now. They need your help."

Meggie hovered reluctantly, obviously torn between showing her aunt around and finishing her painting.

"You go on," Leigh said. "I'll come and look at yours when it's all finished."

"Okay. But don't forget, you hear?"

Leigh suppressed a smile. "I won't."

Meggie ran back to her partners, and Leigh turned to Ms. Carter. When Leigh had asked about her teacher, Meggie had hesitated, then smiled.

"She's beautiful," she'd said.

Meggie was right. Amanda Carter's smooth dark skin glowed with energy; her dark eyes sparkled. Her hair, close cropped, showed a head shaped so perfectly it might have graced a statue. She held out her hand to Leigh.

"Sorry about the informality. We like the summer program to be a bit less structured than the regular school year."

"It looks wonderful," Leigh said, and meant it. In spite of the major project under way, the classroom buzzed with energy and order. Every child had his or her part to play, and Ms. Carter seemed comfortable letting them get on with it.

"I hope you'll decide Sarah can participate. I'd love to have her, and I know it would do my children a great deal of good."

Ms. Carter glanced at her students, and Leigh didn't have any trouble interpreting the look—fierce pride coupled with the anticipation of a challenge.

"Do you know if any of them have ever been around a person with a hearing impairment?"

"No one but Meggie. But she's been so full of enthusiasm about her friend Sarah and how she can talk with her hands that she's built up a lot of interest. I think you'll find most of the children will welcome her."

Facing the classroom as they talked, Leigh could see what Ms. Carter didn't. The curly-haired moppet next to Meggie abruptly reached across and painted a streak along the front of Meggie's painting shirt. Before Leigh could speak, Meggie retaliated with a dot of brick red on the tip of the child's turned-up nose.

Warned either by Leigh's glance or by some teacher's sense, Ms. Carter turned around in time to see the end of it. "Meggie and Emily!" She drew the combatants apart before they could engage in further battle. "The paint goes on the house. If you can't remember that, perhaps you'd like to sit down."

Meggie shot a look of appeal toward Leigh, who kept her expression neutral with an effort. Meggie's lip came out, but her "Yes, Ms. Carter" was a model of decorum.

Emily stamped her foot, red curls flying. "It wasn't my fault! She made me! I'm going to tell my mommy!"

Ms. Carter seemed unimpressed. "In this classroom we follow the rules. You may go and wash up now, Emily."

The look that accompanied the soft-spoken words quelled any further impulse to rebellion. Emily went off with a backward glare at Meggie, and Ms. Carter returned to Leigh.

"Sorry about the interruption. I'm afraid Emily's social skills are a bit lacking sometimes. I was going to say that if you care to participate at any point this afternoon, please feel free. The principal briefed me on your credentials, and I'd be glad to—"

"Oh, no. Thank you." Leigh could only hope that didn't sound too abrupt. "I'm just here to observe, that's all." All she could cope with, she knew. And probably the principal hadn't told Ms. Carter everything there was to know about her.

The afternoon wore on, and Leigh realized staying detached was harder than it sounded. Ms. Carter's energy and expertise had her longing to join in; she knew her input would be welcomed and knew, too, that they'd work well together.

But she stayed firmly on her chair in the corner. Observing—that was her role; not teaching. Just observing.

The social studies lesson over, Ms. Carter gathered the class in a story circle. They wiggled and jostled to get a little closer to her. She waved her hands, and they settled into a snug circle.

"We have a special treat today, boys and girls. Meggie's aunt, Ms. Christopher, is here. Ms. Christopher is a teacher, also. She often works with boys and girls who don't hear well."

Every little face turned in Leigh's direction, and she nodded and smiled, noting the pride on Meggie's face. Her expression seemed to say that she'd really brought something special to show and tell today.

"Ms. Christopher helps children who speak with their hands," Ms. Carter went on. "Perhaps we can persuade her to teach us a few signs."

Leigh's heart thumped. This was just what she had thought she could avoid—getting directly involved. She'd been wrong. She couldn't resist doing this any more than she'd been able to resist Sarah.

She smiled at them, lifting her hands. She was back in a classroom again, and all her firm intentions were lost. This would be joyful and painful probably in equal measure, and she wouldn't miss it for the world.

By the time school was out and she'd dropped Meggie and Mark at home, it was past the hour she usually left Daniel's. She shouldn't go back over there. But the longing to tell him how it had gone was just too intense.

Sarah would thrive in the school program; she just knew she would. She couldn't have a better teacher than Ms. Carter if Leigh had handpicked one. She wanted to share her enthusiasm with Daniel; that was all.

Besides, the bad weather meant that for once he wouldn't be working on the construction. This was the perfect opportunity to talk to him. And if she had any other motives, such as just wanting to see his face again, well…she could ignore them.

The rain had slacked off a bit by the time she reached Daniel's, but sullen clouds hovered, so low they seemed to brush the tops of the palmettos. Out to the southeast, even blacker clouds massed ominously. Leigh scurried into the house, clutching her windbreaker around her.

It was quiet inside. Too quiet. Where was everyone? Then she realized Judith stood at the drop-leaf table in the living room. She had brushed aside the puzzle Leigh and Sarah had been putting together to make room for folding laundry.

Leigh tried for a friendly smile. "It's really quiet in here. Where is everyone?"

Judith folded a small pair of Sarah's shorts. "Sarah's having a nap." She gave Leigh a look that dared her to argue. "I feel she still needs naps."

Telling her that most five-year-olds had outgrown daily naps would only start an argument. Besides, she wasn't here to cross swords with Judith. She just wanted to find Daniel.

"Is Daniel around? There's something I'd like to talk to him about."

Judith raised an eyebrow. "This ridiculous school plan of yours?"

Any hope Leigh might have had that Judith didn't know vanished. She braced herself for the disapproval she could tell was coming.

"I don't think it's ridiculous at all. Sarah would benefit from being around other children."

"Sarah's not ready." Judith's lips firmed into a thin line. "She needs to be protected."

There were a lot of things she could say about overprotection, but Leigh sensed it would do no good. "I guess Daniel will have to make that decision."

Judith planted both fists on the table and leaned forward, eyes blazing. "I know what Sarah's capable of. She can't do this."

Leigh bit her tongue to keep from blurting out something that might alienate her even more. If only she could make Judith understand. The woman could be a wonderful ally if she'd just open her mind to the possibilities.

"Sarah might surprise you. She did very well when I took her to Sunday school, and I think—"

"You!" The word burst out of Judith. "You've only known Sarah a few weeks. I've known her since the day she was born. I know her better than you or Daniel!"

Leigh stiffened. If Daniel constantly had that thrown in his face no wonder he doubted his ability with Sarah. "Daniel is her father. It's his decision to make."

"I won't let you."

Judith took a step toward Leigh. She was so close

that Leigh could feel the anger coming from her in waves.

"I won't let you hurt that child. If I have to, I'll take a leave from my job and stay here to take care of her myself!"

"I—" Leigh closed her mouth on the angry retort she wanted to utter. *Help me, Lord. My temper is about to get the better of me, and I might goad her into doing exactly the wrong thing for Sarah.*

She took a step back. "Excuse me. I don't think the two of us should be discussing this." Not now, not ever. She had to walk away quickly. And she had to talk to Daniel.

Daniel sent a worried glance toward the southeast. He didn't like the looks of that sky. Joe was devoted to the weather channel, but sometimes Daniel just wanted to go with his gut instinct. And right now his gut told him that he'd be in trouble if he didn't get some plywood over that exposed east wall.

"Daniel!"

He jerked around. No one else should be out here. But Leigh stood at the foot of the ladder, wind whipping her yellow jacket around her.

"What are you doing out here? Get inside." Whatever she wanted, he didn't have time for it.

"I've got to talk to you. Can't you quit now?"

He gritted his teeth. Sometimes women had the worst sense of timing in the world. "In case you haven't noticed, there's worse weather coming. We'll talk later."

Leigh shook her head. The wind tore her hood back, tossing her blond hair. "If it's getting worse, you shouldn't be up there. Come down."

"Can't." He dragged a sheet of plywood out. "I've got to get this side covered before the storm hits."

He turned his back on her, concentrating on maneuvering the unwieldy plywood sheet against the wind. Much as he hated to admit it, this wasn't a one-man job. Joe had offered, but no way on earth would he let the old man up here, even on a good day.

He slid the plywood into place, then braced it with his shoulder as he reached for a hammer. It plopped into his hand, and he swung around in surprise, nearly dropping it.

"Careful." Leigh put her hands against the plywood sheet, which buckled when his grip shifted.

He leaned back against it and glared at her. "What are you doing up here? Are you crazy? Get back to the house."

Leigh ignored the order. "Looks like you can use some help. I'll hold—you nail it in place." She smiled. "Nobody in his right mind would trust me with a hammer."

"Nobody in his right mind would let you up here." Daniel planted his fists on his hips. The woman was going to drive him crazy. "Get out, now, before you get hurt. This won't be a picnic when the worst of the wind hits. Some of the construction could come down if I don't get it braced."

Leigh's eyebrows lifted. "Then we'd better get on with it, hadn't we?"

"If you—" He stopped, suddenly realizing how ridiculous it was to be arguing with the help he needed. He felt a smile tug at his mouth.

Leigh grinned, the wind sending wet strands of hair

across her face. "I know—you can do it yourself. But isn't even a poor helper better than none?"

He took the hammer. "Okay, you win. Hold the thing steady."

He positioned the nail and drove it home with two swift strokes. "But if that wind sends you out into the surf, don't expect me to come after you."

She braced herself against the board as he reached for a handful of nails. "If it does, I'll take you with me."

"You won't get the chance—"

The next instant the wind ripped the words from his mouth. A fierce blast of air rippled the plywood. Caught off balance, he struggled to grab it, had a glimpse of Leigh pressing against it with both hands, and then the wind tore it loose and sent them both tumbling backward, the plywood sheet on top of them.

Chapter Twelve

"Leigh!" He shoved the plywood back, his heart pounding. If she was hurt because he'd let her up here… "Are you all right?"

"I'm fine." She pushed at the plywood. "Guess we didn't get that up fast enough."

He grabbed her arm and pulled her to her feet, anger battling the fear he'd felt for her. "Now will you go back to the house?" He had to shout over the rising wind. Maybe he'd have shouted anyway.

"Not unless you're coming, too," she yelled back. "Since you won't, let's get this thing done so we can both get out of here."

Stubbornest woman on earth—he'd bet on it. What was it Joe always said about arguing with a woman? Might as well try to stop the tide.

He picked up the plywood again. "All right." The wind ripped the words from his mouth and plastered his jacket to his skin. "Hold it steady."

The combination of anger and fear did wonders for the speed with which he worked. Leigh, jaw clenched and eyes dark with what he suspected was fear of her own, worked right beside him. In a few minutes they'd nailed the sheets of plywood fast. If that didn't work...well, it was all he could do.

He grabbed Leigh's wet hand. "Come on, let's get out of here. I'll help you down the ladder."

They staggered against the wind to the ladder. He grabbed the top of it, rough wood biting into his fingers. At least it was still there.

Leigh attempted to swing around onto the first rung, fighting the wind. She looked up. "I can't."

He gripped her hand. "Let me go first. I'll help you."

She edged back. He got both feet on the ladder, went down a rung and reached for her.

"Come on. We can do it."

They inched down the ladder, the wind tearing at them like a malevolent force. For a bad moment he pictured Leigh blowing away in a hail of palm fronds. Then his groping foot touched sand.

"Okay." He lifted Leigh down the last few rungs and put his arm around her shoulders. "Let's go."

"Wait a minute." Leigh stopped, shoving sopping hair out of her face. "I need to talk to you. Before we go back to the house."

He looked down at her, torn between anger and laughter. "Haven't you noticed? It's a little wet out here."

"I don't think we can get any wetter than we already are." She shivered, but her jaw set firmly.

"Fine. Great. At least let's get into shelter." He pulled her into what was going to be the entry hall. The wind still howled around the outside, but here they were protected. "What's so important that we can't get dry first?"

She frowned, and he found himself wanting to touch the lines between her brows, smooth them away. He clenched his hands in his pockets.

"When we go back to the house, Judith will be there," Leigh said.

She said it as if he ought to understand. If there was one thing he didn't want to cope with now, it was a battle between Leigh and Judith. But he probably didn't have a choice.

"Okay, shoot. What's she done now?"

Leigh met his eyes, a little defiant, a little embarrassed. "I ran into her when I got back from the school this afternoon. She knew about it, about why I was there and how I want to involve Sarah."

It was his turn to look embarrassed. He shouldn't have let Judith in on it. "Sorry. It just came out. I wasn't discussing you with her."

She shrugged. "I guess she had to know. But she didn't react very well, and I..." Her voice trailed off, and she looked away.

"You wanted to tell me how it went before we got tangled up with Judith again." He leaned against an upright. "Okay, tell me."

Her whole face lit up. There she stood, soaking wet and shivering, and enthusiasm still shone from her like a beacon.

"Daniel, it's perfect for Sarah. Really it is. Ms. Carter is a wonderful teacher, and the program is very relaxed. It's a great opportunity to get Sarah used to being around other kids. She needs that." She put her hand on his arm, her fingers tightening. "Please don't say no. Please give Sarah this chance."

If she'd said to give her this chance, he might have been able to say no. But when she asked for his child, his heart turned to marshmallow.

He tried to buy some time. "What did Judith have to say about it?"

"She hates the idea." Leigh's gaze never wavered. "She thinks Sarah has to be protected from everyone. She even said…"

It looked as if she were editing some of what Judith had said. He could guess. "What?"

"She said if I pursued it, she'd take a leave from her job. She said she'd stay here and look after Sarah herself."

"No." He didn't have to think about his response to that. "That's not going to happen."

"Why isn't it?"

He gave her the answer he knew she waited for. The one she deserved. "Because I trust what you're doing with Sarah. Because you're good for her."

She took a deep breath, her eyes focused on his face. "If you really think that, you'll let me try Sarah at school."

He didn't seem to have any choices left. "All right, Leigh." He gripped her arm. "But you'd better be sure. I don't want Sarah hurt."

Leigh glanced across the car seat at Sarah as they returned from her first time at school two days later. Sarah had a counting paper propped on Leigh's bag in her lap, and she carefully colored in the figures. She paused, searching for a crayon, and then drew a big red circle around the star Ms. Carter had put on the paper.

Leigh touched her shoulder, then pointed to the star. "Nice work," she signed.

Sarah smiled, a glimmer of pride in her eyes.

"Daddy will like that."

Sarah nodded vigorously.

Daniel would like it; Leigh was sure. Nothing bad had happened to Sarah out in the wider world, and she couldn't wait to tell him so. She rode along on a buoyant wave of optimism. Her dreams for Sarah were coming true.

She pulled into the drive. Sarah tucked her crayons neatly back into their box, then slid the box into the blue backpack Leigh had given her. She patted it proudly.

Leigh smiled. It was just like everyone else's; that was what was important. When you were in kindergarten, it was vital to fit in.

The minute they were in the house, Sarah rushed toward the kitchen. She wanted to show her paper to Joe, of course. That was only natural. Maybe the fact that she didn't rush to Aunt Judith showed something about her understanding of Judith's attitude. Regardless of how little she could hear, Sarah had every child's sense of grown-up disapproval.

Leigh looked up at the sound of steps on the curving staircase.

"Where's Sarah?" Judith hurried down the steps. "How was it? Is she upset?"

Leigh took a deep breath and reminded herself that Sarah's aunt loved her. "Sarah's fine. She went out to the kitchen to show her papers to Joe."

"Fine," Judith repeated, frowning. "Is she really? Or are you just saying that because it's what you want to believe?"

Patience, Leigh. Patience. "I'm saying it because it's true. Sarah had a good time. She was a little shy at first, but the other children were very receptive."

Judith looked doubtful, but some of the tension left her face. She really had been worried, Leigh realized, and felt a bit ashamed of her reactions to the woman.

"I..." Judith began, then turned when Sarah came running back into the hall from the kitchen.

Sarah came to a dead halt, glanced down at her papers, then up at her aunt. Speech couldn't have made her feelings any clearer.

To give Judith credit, she understood that as quickly as Leigh had. She smiled, holding out her hand for the papers. "Did you do these? Nice work, Sarah!"

Sarah beamed. Leigh and Judith exchanged a smile over her head, and Leigh felt something in her relax. All right, they weren't going to engage in a pitched battle over this. Good.

Judith stroked Sarah's hair. "You must be tired," she signed. "Let me change your clothes, and then you can take a little nap."

For just an instant Leigh thought...hoped...Sarah would rebel. If she'd assert herself, just once, maybe Judith would realize she was growing up. But Sarah took her aunt's hand and let herself be led up the winding steps.

Leigh fought a wave of disappointment. Well, one battle at a time. Sarah's first day at school had gone well, and Judith hadn't created problems. Maybe she shouldn't expect more from one day.

She started for the kitchen to speak to Joe, then she'd walk down to the construction site and tell Daniel how it had gone. She had hoped he would be waiting to greet Sarah and hear about her day...hoped but hadn't really expected.

A scuffling noise from upstairs stopped her. Something crashed, followed by the sound of scurrying feet.

"No!"

Sarah's unexpected shout had her heart jumping to her throat. Leigh hurried up the steps. What on earth was going on? She raced to the bedroom, then stopped in the doorway.

Sarah, clutching her kitten, stood in the middle of her bedroom. "No!" she shouted again.

"Sarah, it's time for a nap." Judith reached for the kitten. "Let me put the kitty out now so you can rest."

"No." Holding Sassy in a grip the kitten probably didn't appreciate, Sarah evaded her aunt's hand. "Mine," she said firmly. "Sassy mine." She turned, ducked past Leigh and ran down the stairs.

Leigh had hoped Sarah would assert herself, but even she hadn't expected anything quite so dramatic. At the bereft look on Judith's face, Leigh felt her heart go out to the woman. However misguided Judith was, she did love Sarah. She'd just never accepted the fact that Sarah was an independent being. She'd never expected Sarah to have a mind of her own.

"Well."

Judith dropped the T-shirt she'd been holding and turned away, but not before Leigh saw the glitter of tears in her eyes.

"I guess my little Sarah is growing up."

Judith probably wouldn't appreciate sympathy from her. Leigh spoke carefully. "They have a way of doing that."

"I've always tried to do my best for her, you know." Judith clenched her hands.

Leigh took an impulsive step toward her. "I know that. I'm sure Sarah would have been lost without you."

"Perhaps."

Judith stared at the window, but Leigh suspected she wasn't seeing the live oaks and Spanish moss.

"Maybe I took over too much, but Ashley...she didn't seem able to cope."

There wasn't much she could say to that, and Judith apparently didn't expect a response.

"Well." She turned back to Leigh. "Since I'm leaving tonight, I'd better finish packing."

"Tonight? I didn't realize. I thought you weren't leaving until tomorrow."

Judith shook her head. "Joe's driving me to the five o'clock ferry. I can get a good part of my drive done before dark. My parents aren't well, so I have to get back. And things seem to be under control here."

It was a generous admission from someone who'd been opposed to everything she was trying to do. "I hope so," Leigh said softly. "I'll do my best for Sarah—I promise you."

Judith nodded, seemed about to say something, then shook her head and started from the room.

"Judith?"

Judith paused, and Leigh asked the question that had been bothering her from the first day she'd spent with Sarah. "Do you have any idea what the doll and cradle mean to Sarah? I've never understood that."

"Putting the baby to bed." Judith's mouth tightened. "I don't see what difference it makes now. You already know everything you need to about our family.''

"Anything you tell me that helps me understand Sarah...as you said, you know her as well as anyone.''

Judith gave Leigh a measured look, as if she were trying to decide how genuine that statement was. Apparently whatever she saw in Leigh's eyes satisfied her, because she managed a reluctant nod.

"Ashley didn't spend much time with Sarah in the last year or two." Judith's voice flattened as Daniel's did when he spoke of Ashley. "I just wanted Sarah to know she was loved. I told her about how, when she was little, her mommy would tuck her into bed and sing to her. I didn't expect—'' Judith stopped, putting her hand to her mouth.

Hurt choked Leigh for a little girl so desperate for her mother's love that she'd try to re-create it with a baby doll.

"No," Leigh said softly. "No, you couldn't expect that. No one would."

While Judith packed, Leigh took Sarah down to the beach. Arms widespread, Sarah skipped along the sand ahead of her, dancing into the wind as if she were a sandpiper. Leigh took a breath of air swept free of the humidity of the last weeks.

The storm, leaving, had blessed them with some perfect golden days. The air was so clear she half expected to see all the way to Ireland. The beach, scoured clean, stretched ahead of them, inviting them to run, to celebrate. Maybe Sarah felt that, too, and she spun in dizzying circles.

Judith's departure swept something else clean. Her coming just when she did had interrupted whatever had been happening the night of the picnic. Those moments when Leigh and Daniel had been so close— would they go back to that now? And if they did, what would happen between them?

Nothing, she told herself firmly. She'd be leaving the island by the end of the summer, so there couldn't be a future for them. She had a job interview in Savannah coming up, and if that didn't pan out, something else would.

Besides, Daniel didn't really want anything to happen between them. That night, those moments alone on his boat—they had been a mistake, and he realized it as well as she did.

Daniel had made it clear that he wasn't ready, probably would never be ready, to rely on anyone but himself again. The thought brought such real pain that she actually put her hand on her chest.

Help him, Lord. The cry came from her heart. *Even if he's never ready for a real relationship with a woman, let him know, somehow, that he can always rely on You.*

The house was quiet, too quiet, Leigh thought. Joe had left to take Judith to the ferry, before going to a potluck supper at his church. Leigh had agreed to stay and have supper with Sarah so Daniel could catch up on his work.

Sarah, restless, wandered around the living room. She'd already teased the kitten until he'd taken refuge under the buffet and refused to come out.

Overtired, Leigh thought, and felt a pang of guilt. Maybe she hadn't thought through the toll school would take on Sarah. Coping with a new situation, feeling uncertain about what to do, had to be difficult.

Sarah probably sensed that everyone else had an advantage she didn't.

Leigh glanced at the clock. She couldn't put Sarah to bed yet. It was too early, and besides, she hadn't had a chance to see much of her daddy this whole day.

"I know what, Sarah." Leigh switched on the radio and turned the dial, looking for music. "Let's dance."

She set the radio on the floor so Sarah could feel the vibrations. "See?" She grasped Sarah's hands and moved in time to the loud, steady beat. "Dancing."

Sarah's face lit up as she understood. "Dancing," she signed back. Her feet moved in time to the music, and they danced around the room. Sarah tipped back her head and laughed aloud as they spun.

Leigh felt as she had when Sarah had twirled on the beach, as free as the wind. This was what Sarah needed, this sense of freedom. She swung her around dizzyingly, loving it, laughter bubbling. Then she stumbled to a halt.

Daniel stood in the doorway, watching them. His dark hair curled damply around his face, as if he'd just come from the shower, and his T-shirt clung to his broad shoulders.

He lifted an eyebrow. "Did I miss my invitation to the ball?"

"I guess you did." She could feel her cheeks warm just from his glance. She twirled Sarah over to him. "Here's the prettiest girl at the ball, all ready to dance with you."

He took a few steps with Sarah, then glanced at Leigh. "How does she...?"

"She's hearing the music, a little." Leigh smiled.

"That's why it's so loud, but I figured there was no one here to disturb. And she's picking up the vibrations through the floor, too." She danced a step or two to the beat. "Can't you feel it?"

His gaze clung to her face for a long moment. "Yes," he said softly, and his look brought the blood surging to her cheeks again. "I can feel it."

She retreated to the radio and sank onto the rug next to it. She fiddled with the volume as an excuse not to look at him. When she glanced up again, he was spinning Sarah around the room. The two faces, so alike with their dark eyes sparkling, were lit with laughter. Her heart jolted uncomfortably at the sight.

The song ended, and a slow, soft ballad came on. She reached to change the station, but Sarah ran across and grabbed her hand. She tugged at her, and Leigh got to her feet, not sure what Sarah had in mind. Sarah smiled, then led her across the room to Daniel.

"Looks like Sarah thinks it's our turn to dance together." His voice was soft, husky. He held out his hand, an invitation in his dark eyes. "May I have this dance?"

Leigh looked at his hand. Sarah nudged her forward. Then, frustrated at Leigh's hesitation, she grabbed her hand and put it in Daniel's. She stepped back with a satisfied smile.

"My daughter knows what she wants." Daniel's fingers closed warmly around hers. "All right, Cinderella?"

She nodded. "All right." She rested her hand lightly on his shoulder. Not lightly enough, she realized. Being this close to him was dangerous to her peace of mind.

It was just a dance, she told herself desperately. Just a dance. Trouble was, she didn't believe it herself.

"If I'm Cinderella, does that make you the prince?"

He pulled her a little closer into the circle of his arms, his hand warm at her waist. "It's either that or a frog. Take your choice."

"Actually, I'm rather fond of frogs. Especially since Mark told me about all the insects they eat."

"He did, did he?" Daniel's voice was low in her ear.

She had to keep babbling, because if she didn't he might suspect how her heart was pounding. "In vivid detail, with pictures."

"He's quite a kid." His hand moved slowly on her waist, drawing her nearer. "Special. Like his aunt."

There wasn't anything she could say that wouldn't sound as if she took his comment seriously. She ought to say something...anything...light, but she'd suddenly become tongue-tied.

Daniel didn't seem to expect a response. He hummed softly in her ear, and the romantic words and music mixed with his warm breath across her cheek.

She closed her eyes, giving herself up to the sensation... Daniel, the music, the quiet room. The feeling that she'd come home.

She could hear her heartbeat. Or was that Daniel's?

This was dangerous; it was so dangerous. It gave her visions of something that could never be...visions of a life in which Daniel opened up, trusted again. A life in which three people could become a family.

It can't be, she reminded herself. Daniel didn't want that, not any longer. Not after what had happened with Ashley. If she gave her heart to him, he'd break it, because he was determined not to have the kind of love she needed for a lifetime of happiness.

Love. Was she really using that word in connection with Daniel? She glanced up, unwary, and his lips brushed her cheek with the movement. Her skin tingled, and her breath caught in her throat.

Love. She was falling in love with Daniel Gregory.

Chapter Thirteen

Daniel saw her eyes darken suddenly, felt her stiffen in his arms. She pulled away, almost stumbling as she stepped back. He could feel the tension pouring from her in waves.

He was a fool.

She'd let him know that night on the beach that she wasn't going to settle for less than a real relationship, and he just didn't think he had that to offer anymore.

But he wanted to…the realization struck him like a two-by-four. He wanted to be able to love that way. Leigh Christopher, with her sweet warmth and her dogged determination to do what was right, had made him want it again, even if it was impossible.

"Sorry," he said, not sure what he was sorry for but somehow knowing it was the only thing to say. He tried for a light touch. "Did Cinderella hear the clock strike?"

"Something like that." Her voice sounded breathless. "There's something... I remembered something I need to talk to you about."

He realized she wasn't signing, and foreboding clutched at him. It had to be something bad if she wasn't signing so that Sarah could be part of the conversation. Had he ruined things entirely? Had he lost Sarah someone she desperately needed?

"What is it?" His words sounded harsh to his ears.

"You know I've been sending out résumés."

That wasn't what he expected, and he stared at her.

Leigh frowned, green eyes troubled. "Well, I've finally had a response. I've been called about a job in Savannah. They want me to come tomorrow."

The surprise sent him a step back. It shouldn't have been a shock, but it was. He'd known all along what she wanted; she hadn't made a secret of it. But he'd deluded himself that what he offered—spending her days in his house, caring for his child—was enough for her. His stomach churned, and he tried not to think what this meant for Sarah, for him.

"So you're leaving."

"No!" She reached out as if to touch him, then pulled back her hand. "No."

"That's how it sounds." He couldn't seem to stamp the bitter flavor from the words.

"It's just an interview, that's all. I'll miss my time with Sarah tomorrow. Then I'll be back."

"And if they offer you the job?" He didn't need to know what the job was. It didn't matter. Anyone who had a chance to hire Leigh and didn't was an idiot. They'd offer it and she'd take it, because that was what she wanted. She was stubbornly determined not to do what she did best.

"I'm sure they have loads of people to interview.

And I don't know if it's the right job for me anyway." Leigh spread her hands wide, palms up. "How can I know that until I talk to them?"

"If it's right, if they offer it, what then?" He hammered the phrases back at her, trying to blank out the thought of doing without her. "You'll walk away."

Her eyes widened. "Daniel, I wouldn't leave you and Sarah now. Not with six weeks of summer left. I promise. I'd find a way to work it out. I'd—"

He shook his head. "Forget it." He had to force himself to smile, to sound rational. "Look, if it's the right job for you, you'll take it. It's as simple as that. After all, we both knew this might happen from the beginning. You don't owe us anything."

"It's not a question of owing. It's a question of what's right." Her soft lips compressed. "I won't desert Sarah. I promise."

Promises. He'd relied on promises before, and he knew just where that led. He didn't have any claim on Leigh...didn't want to have any claim on her. His gut twisted at that, but he ignored it.

She'd leave. That was the way it was.

He turned away, then realized that Sarah was watching them, her face strained and apprehensive. He lifted her in his arms and held her close, then looked past his daughter at Leigh. He forced a smile.

"Do what's right for you, Leigh. We'll understand."

Leigh lingered in the late-afternoon heat on the deck at Jamie's house several days later. She was reluctant to go inside. Jamie would ask, as she always did, how things were with Sarah and Daniel.

Leigh rested her elbows on the deck rail and stared

at the elegant white shape of an egret in the salt marsh. Sarah was fine; no doubt about that. They'd decided on three days a week at school to start, and Sarah loved her days at school and moped on the days she stayed home. She'd made wonderful progress.

Unfortunately, things weren't so wonderful with Daniel. In fact, things had been different between them ever since the night she told him about the job interview. To be exact, since the night they danced, the night she realized she was falling in love with him.

She pressed her hands to her cheeks. She hadn't meant to let herself feel that way, not about Daniel. Love had crept up on her when she wasn't noticing, and by the time she knew, it was too late.

Had he guessed? Was that why he'd been so distant for the past several days? Or was that simply his reaction to her job interview? She didn't know, and she was afraid to find out. She was afraid of what the answer might be.

Daniel Gregory wasn't right for her. That was the bottom line, whatever she felt. He'd as much as said it, hadn't he? He'd tried love, tried trust, and they had failed. He wouldn't try again. No matter how much he might want to be with her, he wouldn't…maybe couldn't…give her the commitment that she had to have to build a future on.

Oh, Lord, why did You let me meet him, why did You let me fall in love with him, if it was never to be?

The question tore from her heart, but in the next instant Leigh was ashamed of it. Loving Daniel, even if he didn't love her back, had taught her so much. It had shown her what kind of man she could give her heart to. It had shown her that she couldn't settle for second best, even if it meant doing without entirely.

Leigh pressed her hands against the rail, feeling the rough wood bite into her palms. She couldn't change what happened, or rather what didn't happen, with Daniel. The only thing she could do was her job, and that meant trying her hardest to get the best for Sarah.

Sarah. She was doing so well. Oh, there were problems, frustrations. Every child at school didn't welcome her, but that would be true for a hearing child, as well.

Each time they went into the classroom it reinforced Leigh's feeling that this was what Sarah needed: to have the security of her father and her home and to go to school here, where she had that support. The difficulty still lay in convincing Daniel.

The summer was running out. She had to do something, and do it soon.

The possibility lay at hand. She clenched the rail, indecision eating at her. Sarah could participate with the other children in the open-house program. Amanda Carter had been lobbying for that all week, but Leigh had held back, not convinced Sarah was ready.

If Sarah did take part and it worked out well, that could go a long way toward convincing Daniel. If he saw his daughter in the program, just like everyone else, that would do it if anything would.

And if she was wrong? If Sarah wasn't ready and it went badly? Leigh bit her lip. *Show me what to do, Lord. I need to know.*

But no sureness blossomed in her mind, answering her. Time was running out, and she had to make a decision.

"Leigh!" Jamie swung the door open. "What are you doing out here in the heat?"

"I'm on my way in." Leigh pushed herself away from the rail and followed her sister into the kitchen. "Have a good day?"

Jamie grimaced as she pulled the door closed behind them. "So-so. All anyone could talk about all day was this latest tropical storm, and it's barely started to form. If I hear one more weather forecast, I'm going to scream."

"That's what you get for living on an island. The weather forms fifty percent of the conversation." Leigh crossed to the sink and reached for a glass.

"More like ninety percent during hurricane season," Jamie said. "By the way, there was a call for you earlier."

The odd note in Jamie's voice spun her around. "A call? What about?"

Jamie frowned, her gaze meeting Leigh's. "It was about that job in Savannah. I wrote it down on the phone pad. You're supposed to call them back." She hesitated. "Sounds to me as if they want you."

Leigh snatched up the phone pad and read the brief message, mind whirling. When she hadn't heard anything within a couple of days, she'd pretty much given up. And now this.

"You really think they're going to offer?"

Jamie shrugged. "I don't know why else they'd call. So, what are you going to do?"

"I don't know." She really didn't. Much as she'd thought about this, she didn't. "It's a good position. And I wouldn't be too far from you."

"But it's not teaching."

Leigh closed her eyes briefly against a stab of pain. "No, it's not teaching. That's the point, remember?"

"I'd hoped—" Jamie stopped, leaning against the counter, frowning. "Honestly, Leigh, hasn't your experience with Sarah told you something? You were meant to be a teacher."

"Was I?" She remembered Tommy and shook her head. "I always thought so, but look how it turned out."

"Leigh, that wasn't your fault. Your only crime was trying to help a child."

The familiar pain gripped her heart. "I let everyone down... Tommy most of all."

Jamie's eyebrows lifted. "Everyone? What everyone?"

"Mom, Dad, you." Leigh swallowed hard. She'd thought this for months; she'd just never managed to say it. "Everyone sacrificed so I could have the education I wanted. Don't you think I know that? I told myself I'd pay all of you back by being the best teacher I could be. And then I got into a mess." She turned away, not wanting to see Jamie's face. "Don't you think I know how disappointed you all were in me?"

"Leigh Anne Christopher!" Jamie grabbed her arm and spun her around. "That's just nonsense, and if you don't know it, you should. We sacrificed to send you to school because we wanted to. Because your vocation was a God-given gift!"

"If that's true..." All of a sudden, tears choked her voice. "If that's true, why did it turn out so badly? Why did people have to get hurt?"

"Oh, honey." Jamie's arms went around her, warm and comforting. "You couldn't control what those

other people did. You were just trying to help a child.
We understand that.''

She was acting like a fool, blubbering about it after
all this time, but she couldn't seem to help herself.
''I feel so guilty. If I hadn't been so sure I was right,
if only I'd talked it over with my supervisor...''

''Leigh.'' Jamie's eyes were bright with unshed
tears. ''If you did make a mistake, if there was something you should have done differently, haven't you
asked for forgiveness?''

''Of course I have!'' God knew how much time
she'd spent on her knees since it had happened.

Jamie blotted Leigh's tears. ''Honey, if you've
asked for God's forgiveness, why haven't you ever
accepted it?''

The question fell into Leigh's mind. It resonated,
sending out circles of questions, answers, understanding.

Could she have been hanging on to her guilt, unwilling to accept forgiveness? Thinking she knew better than God did?

Jamie patted her cheek. ''The big-sister lecture is
over. Just don't keep beating yourself up, okay?''

Leigh tried to smile. ''Okay.''

''Well.'' Jamie turned away, assuming her usual
brisk air. ''Enough rampant emotion. I need to get
these salads finished for the crab boil tonight and you
need to return that call.''

Leigh nodded, went to the telephone, placed the
call.

The personnel officer detailed the terms of the job
offer, and they were better than Leigh had hoped.
Then...

''Of course we'll need you to start right away.''

"But…" Leigh took a breath. "During my interview, I pointed out that I wouldn't be available until September." Sarah. She had promises to keep to Sarah.

"I'm afraid that's not possible." The woman's tone hardened. "You're our first choice, but if you're not willing to start now, we'll simply have to go to our next candidate."

Tell me what to do, Lord. Leigh listened to the calm certainty that pooled in her mind.

"I'm sorry," she said. "I guess the job isn't for me."

When she hung up the phone, she turned to meet Jamie's hopeful gaze.

Leigh shook her head. "Don't jump to conclusions just because I didn't take this job."

"Of course not." Jamie dumped macaroni into a colander, suddenly busy.

"I just couldn't desert Sarah now. I have an obligation to her. That's all." At least, she told herself that was all.

"Auntie Leigh! Look at the pony rides!" Meggie dragged Leigh by the hand as they walked down to the beach for the community picnic that night. "I want to ride a pony! I want Sarah to ride a pony, too. Where is she?"

"I don't know if they're coming, honey." She'd asked Daniel and gotten nothing but a shrug and a noncommittal response.

Meggie pouted. "I want her to. And I want to ride the pony anyway."

Josh caught her by the hand before she could dart off toward the beguiling ponies. "Later, sugar.

There's a crab boil going on over there, and I want my supper. Eat first, then check out the rides.''

They followed the crowd toward the long picnic tables, where Jamie unloaded the salads she'd brought. The paper-covered tables groaned under the weight of dishes loaded with one island specialty after another.

Jamie elbowed Leigh and pointed to one large yellow crock. "That's Mrs. Culpepper's broccoli salad. Don't miss it. Nobody knows exactly what she puts in it, but it's fantastic.''

"Broccoli!" Josh wrinkled his nose. "Lead me to the sweet-potato pie, thanks.''

"You're going to look like a sweet-potato pie if you don't watch out.'' Jamie tickled him, and he retaliated by sweeping her into a bear hug.

Leigh watched them, a hollow feeling forming in the pit of her stomach. It wasn't hunger, or at least not the kind of hunger that any amount of broccoli salad or sweet-potato pie could satisfy. She was hungry for the kind of love they shared, and it seemed more and more likely that, for her, it wasn't to be.

"Look, Auntie Leigh! It's Sarah!''

She spun around at Meggie's words, heart suddenly pounding in her ears. Sarah, Joe and Daniel worked their way through the crowd toward them.

At the sight of Daniel, she knew she'd been kidding herself. It wasn't just a love like Jamie and Josh's that she wanted. It was a love like that with Daniel. And it wasn't going to happen.

The moment he saw Leigh, Daniel knew why he'd come tonight. He'd been telling himself he was just giving in to the combined pressure brought by Joe and Sarah, but that wasn't it. Or, at least, not all of it. He'd come because he wanted to see Leigh again.

Idiot that he was, he couldn't resist the impulse. Since the night they'd danced, he'd been keeping a careful distance, and he wasn't sure any more whether he was protecting her or himself.

One thing he knew as soon as he saw the way she softened at the sight of him: keeping his distance wasn't doing any good. He was past protecting. Even knowing that she'd leave, even knowing that he could never give her what she needed, he still couldn't stop wanting to be near her.

Sarah tugged his hand as she caught sight of Meggie, pulling him toward the others. *Careful,* he told himself. *Just be careful. No more playing with fire where Leigh Christopher is concerned.*

"Daniel!" Josh leaned across the laden table to shake hands. "Hey, Joe. Sarah. Grab a plate and join us."

Careful, Daniel reminded himself. But he couldn't refuse to join them, and he didn't want to. "Sounds great." He greeted the others, smiling as Sarah and Meggie climbed on the picnic bench together. "Leigh. How are things going? I haven't had much chance to talk to you lately." *Because I've avoided being in the same room with you.*

"Fine." Leigh seemed to concentrate on filling her plate. "Sarah's doing great."

"And you?" He lowered his voice, knowing he really wanted to ask about the job, not sure he should.

"Fine," she said again. Then she shook her head slightly, as if shaking off an argument with herself. "There's something I want to tell you."

He put an ear of corn on his plate and tried to sound as though it meant nothing at all. "Shoot."

"They offered me the job in Savannah, with the condition that I start right away."

That was it. "So you'll be leaving."

"No." She looked up at him, and the food nearly slid from her plate. He reached out to save it, and their hands collided.

"No? What do you mean, no?"

"I turned them down." She drew her plate, and her hand, away. "I decided it wasn't what I want."

"Well." His brain was suddenly scrambled. What exactly did she mean by that? That she didn't want that particular job? Or that she didn't want to leave?

The questions hovered on his tongue. But he didn't have the right to ask. That was a question you could ask if you wanted a commitment, not if you were dedicated to running from one.

"That's good news," he said finally. "Sarah would really miss you if you went." Stupid, inadequate words. He'd made it sound as if he didn't care at all.

Something—a shadow—crossed those green eyes. She put a careful step between them, as if protecting herself.

"I'd miss her, too."

"I meant—" He stopped. Anything he said would make it worse.

Well, he'd certainly handled that badly. He followed the others to a table. Maybe he'd better stick to things he knew something about.

He nodded toward the new bridge construction out in the sound, the two halves reaching toward each other across blue-gray water.

"Looks out of place, doesn't it?"

Josh turned, crab leg in hand, and gazed across the sound. "Going to seem awful funny just getting in a car and driving over there."

"Change everything." Joe shook his head mournfully. "Won't be islanders anymore."

"Why not?" Leigh turned to him, eyes wide. "What do you mean?"

Joe shrugged, cutting corn off the cob with the precision of a surgeon. "Seen it other places. Soon as the bridge comes in, everything changes. What makes us special, different—it'll just get lost."

"I hope not." Leigh reached out to put her hand over his worn one for a moment. "I really hope not."

Jamie cleared her throat. "Enough gloomy talk." She gestured toward the children. "Little ears, remember? Besides, we'll still be the same, no matter what." She turned to Daniel. "So, are you going to the open house at school this week?"

He glanced at Leigh. "I don't think I knew about it. Am I going, Leigh?"

That sounded more intimate than he'd intended. Almost as if he were a husband consulting his wife about their social calendar. Probably nobody else noticed, but Leigh's cheeks flushed slightly.

"Yes, I hope so." Her eyes met his, and there seemed to be a challenge in them. "You have to come and see Sarah take part."

He nodded. "I guess I am."

Eating, then games, then finally dancing and fireworks. That was the inevitable progression of the island picnic, had been for a hundred years probably. They stayed with Leigh's family because it would have been awkward to go off on their own. At least, that's what Daniel told himself.

Every time he watched his Sarah jump on a ride or run to look at something, his heart seemed to clench. Wasn't this what he'd always wanted for her: to be accepted, to have friends? Why was it so scary? He kept waiting, tensed, for something to go wrong. And when she and Meggie went on the ponies...

"Relax."

Leigh touched his arm lightly, then drew her hand away. Too late. Her touch reverberated along his skin.

"I am relaxed."

She lifted her eyebrows. "Liar."

"Okay." He grinned. "But I am letting her do it. I'm not out there hanging on to her."

"You'd look a little silly on the back of that pony."

"I guess I would at that." Something in him really did relax then. Maybe it was just having Leigh smile at him again. "My little girl's taking on a lot of firsts all at once. I get to be a little protective, don't I?"

"Just a little."

The girls scrambled down from the ponies and ran back to them, excited, Sarah's hands flying. He resisted the impulse to pick her up. She was a big girl now. He couldn't treat her like a baby.

A preliminary blare came from the loudspeaker. Sarah spun around, hands going to her ears. Then the music started, and she smiled. She grabbed Meggie's hand and tugged her toward the improvised dance floor.

"Looks like dancing is almost as popular as ponies." He walked beside Leigh toward the dancers.

"Just about."

He could hear the reserve in her voice and knew she was remembering just what he was. The two of them, arms around each other, as they swayed to soft music. The moment when his lips brushed her skin and felt it warm in response.

Josh led Jamie onto the dance floor and waved to them. "Come on, you two. Get with it."

He almost turned to her then, almost slid his arm around her waist and led her onto the floor. Almost.

He took a careful step back, before he could give in to the urge to take her in his arms.

She swung away, holding out her hand to Mark.

"Come on, Mark. Let's show them how it's done."

Chapter Fourteen

Leigh discovered she was holding her breath as the kindergarten class marched onstage for rehearsal. *Breathe,* she told herself firmly, and went to help Amanda Carter get the children lined up.

Amanda shook her head. "Oh, how I hate performances. Your best kids always get stage fright, and somebody invariably decides to be sick at a crucial moment."

"It comes with the territory, remember?" Leigh put a restraining hand on the boy who'd decided the stage steps were perfect for jumping. "The parents love to see their darlings perform."

"Only if they look cute and don't goof up." Amanda clapped her hands. "Everyone with a speaking part in the skit, come to the front. Everyone else, take your place in the back."

Leigh watched Sarah wiggle to the back row. "Look cute and don't goof up," Amanda had said, and that was about the size of it. In the skit, that was all Sarah had to do. As long as she stayed in her assigned spot and clapped at the news that the colonists' ship had arrived from England, she'd be fine.

The folk dance sequence—that would be the tricky part. If Sarah could just do that the way they'd practiced it…nothing would go wrong, Leigh assured herself. Sarah would be fine, Daniel would be impressed and the whole situation would work out just the way she'd prayed it would.

"All right, dancers." Amanda clapped her hands again. "Let's give this a try."

"And try to remember left and right," Leigh murmured.

Amanda glanced at her and rolled her eyes. Leigh knew just what she was thinking. Amanda had said from the beginning that this dance was too difficult for the kindergartners.

But one of the mothers, who also happened to be president of the PTO, had supplied the music and the enthusiasm. So they were doing it, or at least trying to. So far they'd done it right only once.

Leigh started the tape after setting the player on the stage floor so that Sarah could feel the vibrations as the music played.

One step, two, three…

"No, I'm afraid not." Amanda stepped in when the third complicated step resulted in a hopeless tangle of little bodies. "Let's try it again. Jason, remember that this is your right hand."

Leigh rewound the tape, and the music started again. The children began to move. Leigh held her breath. *Please, please don't let Sarah make a mistake.*

That time they got about halfway through before some unscheduled pushing took place. Emily, red curls bouncing, swung on Meggie, who pushed right back.

Leigh suppressed a smile. Emily should have figured out by now that Meggie gave as good as she got, but she continued to agitate. Was she jealous of Meggie? Leigh wasn't sure what the problem was.

"Meggie made me miss the step!" Emily declared. "She did!"

"You missed it all by your own self," Meggie said loftily. She took Sarah's hand. "Me and Sarah are good dancers."

Amanda rearranged the small bodies. "Let's try it again," she said, her tone tactful. "Ms. Christopher, will you rewind the tape?"

This time they almost got through the entire dance. Suddenly the sound cut out on the player. Sarah, lost without the rhythm, bumped into Meggie. Her small face clouded with distress.

"It's okay." Meggie patted her, looking and sounding for all the world like Jamie. "You didn't do anything wrong, Sarah."

Leigh resisted the urge to go to Sarah. It was better, far better, if Sarah coped with Meggie's help. She busied herself getting the tape player going again. When she looked up, Sarah was back in her place, clouds gone.

"Once more," Amanda said, and Leigh could hear the slightest frustration in her voice. "It's almost time to leave, so let's get it right this time."

This time, astoundingly, they were perfect.

"Good job, everyone!" Amanda clapped. "Do it that well for your parents tomorrow, all right?"

The children scampered off the stage, and Sarah ran to Leigh, eyes shining.

"I'm a good dancer," she signed.

"Yes, you are." Leigh hugged her, then Meggie, her heart overflowing with joy that Sarah could finally come up with such a positive statement about herself. "You're both good dancers. I'm proud of you."

And hopeful, she added silently. Tomorrow Daniel would see how well his daughter fit in. Tomorrow he'd understand Leigh's hopes for her and begin looking at her future in a whole new way.

Leigh slowed as she drove past the general store on the way home. The big plate-glass window in front sported a starburst of tape, and old Mr. Conyers directed two teenage boys as they removed his awning.

Leigh's stomach clenched, and she switched the car radio on. She didn't have to search for the report. Instead of music, the radio featured the latest update on Tropical Storm Eleanor.

The storm had set its course for Puerto Rico, the announcer said, and residents there braced for the worst. The current projected track had it headed straight for the southeast coast after that.

Leigh peered down the street. Nobody seemed to be panicking, but several other windows were taped. She pulled into a parking place. It began to look as if, ready or not, she was going to experience her first hurricane.

Sarah glanced up from her coloring, surprised at the unexpected stop.

"Let's go in the store," Leigh said. "I need to get some things."

Inside, the bread shelf was already running low. Mr. Conyers followed Leigh and eyed the shelf.

"Don't know why people think they're going to

eat so much bread when there's a big one coming.''
He grinned. '''Course, I'm glad to sell it to them. You
ladies want some bread?''

Leigh shook her head, smiling. ''I'm sure my sister's already prepared. But I could use a flashlight for
myself. Oh, and one for my friend Sarah, too. And
some extra batteries.''

He put them on the counter, then carefully took a
red licorice from the countertop jar and held it out to
Sarah. ''There you go, sweet thing.''

Sarah's eyes widened. Her hand moved outward
from her mouth before she took the candy.

''Thank you,'' Leigh said. ''That means 'thank
you.'''

The old man chuckled. ''Well, I'll be.'' He repeated the gesture. ''What d'you know. I've learned
something new.''

Sarah smiled back at him and sucked on the end
of the licorice whip.

They'd better get home and see if Daniel needed
any help preparing for the storm. A queasy feeling
took control of Leigh's stomach. She'd never seen a
hurricane, except in the movies. What must it be like
to live through one?

When they got to the house, they found Daniel and
Joe standing outside. Arguing.

''It's not going to be that bad.'' The tone of Daniel's voice suggested that the argument had been going on for some time. ''Tape is enough. We don't
need to put up the plywood. Besides, it probably
won't even hit.''

Joe planted his hands on his hips. ''I've seen
storms and I've seen *storms*. And I reckon this one's
coming.''

The two of them glared at each other with identically stubborn expressions, and Leigh held back the urge to laugh.

"Having a disagreement, gentlemen?"

Daniel swung toward her in the swift movement that never failed to make her heart do a little double-quick step.

"I didn't hear you coming." Sarah ran to him, and he gave her a hug. "What's that?"

Sarah proudly clicked her new flashlight on and off, showing it to him.

"We decided we should be prepared for the storm. If it comes," Leigh added hastily.

Daniel shook his head. "This old man is convinced he knows best."

"I've seen storms..." Joe began.

"And you've seen *storms,*" Daniel finished for him. "I know, I know. Okay, we tape the windows today, and I'll get out the plywood. There's time enough to put it up later, when the weather service has a better handle on where landfall will be. Then I've got to get to the construction." Worry furrowed his forehead. "That's a heck of a lot more vulnerable."

"You go ahead," Leigh said. "I can tape windows with Joe."

"Maybe you ought to get home to your sister's...."

"Please. You know Jamie. She's prepared for anything short of the Great Flood." Leigh put her hand on Sarah's shoulder. "Sarah and I will help Joe. We'll be fine."

The rest of the afternoon passed to the constant accompaniment of the radio. Joe carried it with him everywhere, seemingly convinced that if he didn't listen all the time, he might miss the crucial warning. They taped, put away everything that was loose and might blow around, drew buckets of water.

Leigh, passing the telephone at some point that afternoon, stopped. Amanda Carter had done a lesson on using the phone, and obviously Sarah had taken it to heart. The paper taped to the phone table bore Leigh's name and number, printed in Sarah's wavy letters.

Leigh blinked away sudden tears. Sarah might never use the phone to call her, but Ms. Carter had said to list important numbers by the phone, and so she had.

Joe lined kerosene lanterns on the kitchen table like so many soldiers, filling and checking each one.

"Power's going to go off, sure as you're born. We'll be glad of these before the night's over."

But by the time Leigh was getting ready to go home, the forecasts were less ominous.

"You see, old man?" Daniel came in from the construction in time to hear the announcement. "Eleanor's going to blow herself out before she ever hits land. It's a false alarm, like most watches."

"We'll see what we'll see." Joe shook his head. "Never trust a hurricane."

"Better safe than sorry." The nervous energy on which Leigh had been running all day seeped away, and she realized how tired she was. "At least we'll get the open-house program in tomorrow. I don't know what Amanda Carter would do if she had to get the children ready all over again."

Daniel nodded. "Looks that way." He smiled. "And if the storm does come, everybody will be too busy to worry about it."

Leigh dropped a kiss on Sarah's head. "Well, I'll be off, then. I'll see you tomorrow."

Throughout the evening the news continued to improve. Tropical Storm Eleanor was a washout, the newscaster declared. All her early threat had been just so much bluster. She'd dawdle herself to nothing in the northern Caribbean.

"Looks like that's it, then." Jamie finally switched the news off at around eleven. She yawned. "We'd better get to bed. You've got a big day tomorrow, with that program at school."

Leigh nodded, her stomach tightening in an apprehension that was somehow worse than the threat of any storm. Tomorrow, come what may, Daniel would see what his daughter could do.

Daniel pulled into the school parking lot, stopped the car and realized that his stomach was tied in knots. Somehow he could handle whatever life threw at *him*, but his daughter...well, that was another story.

He had a moment of panic. Why had he let himself be talked into letting her do this?

Because Leigh thought she could, that was the answer. And because he'd come to depend on Leigh's opinion far more than he'd ever have thought possible just a few short weeks ago.

He joined the other parents heading into the building. Sarah could do this. She could. She'd be fine, and she was going to look out into the crowd and see that her daddy was there, supporting her.

The cinder-block cafeteria, bright with posters, was a far cry from the elementary school he'd gone to. No cafeteria there at all. You brought your lunch, assuming your folks had something to send. Sometimes he'd had something; sometimes he'd had to pretend he'd already eaten. Mostly he'd passed off what he had to his brother and sisters, saying he wasn't hungry.

His stomach tightened again. When she talked about school, Leigh pictured a place entirely different from his memories. She probably couldn't imagine going to school hungry. Or coming home with a black eye more often than not because somebody had teased your little sister for wearing a dress from the charity box.

Nobody knew better than he did how cruel kids could be. He didn't want to think about anybody turning that kind of cruelty on his child.

Josh waved from a seat toward the front, and Daniel made his way toward him and Jamie. Half the island seemed to be here today, or at least anybody who had children or grandchildren.

"Hey, Daniel." Josh slid over on the cafeteria bench to make room. "How's it going? You get ready for Eleanor?"

"Looks like she's not going to pay us a visit after all." Daniel sat down. "Can't say I'm sorry."

"A good storm—" Josh began, but Jamie shushed him.

"They're starting," she whispered.

Daniel tried to focus on the stage, where the principal was making welcoming remarks, but his attention was distracted. The kindergartners filed in to the side of the room. Apparently they were first. Thank goodness he wouldn't have to wait this out too long.

Leigh came in with them, surrounded by a cluster of children, and his heart gave an uncomfortable thump. No matter how many times he saw her, it didn't get old. He still found his eyes lingering on her, drinking in that soft, sunny presence.

Man, you've got it bad.

It was no use, he reminded himself. But that didn't mean he could quit looking. Well, anyone could look. But not just anyone could interpret that faint frown between her brows, that slight apprehension clouding her clear eyes. He could see the tension in her from across the room.

She looked up suddenly, as if she felt his gaze on her across all those feet of polished floor. Her eyes met his, met and clung. She gave him a small, private smile, then turned back to the children.

He let out a frustrated breath. Frustrated, that was a good word for it. Frustration gnawed at him every time he was in the same room with the woman. He wanted to close the gap between them, wanted to go right up to her, to say...

To say what? That he was falling in love with her? That he wanted her in his life? That maybe, just maybe, he could find a way to trust enough to make it work? The terrifying thought lodged in his mind and tied his guts in knots.

"Our first performers will be the kindergarten group, under the direction of Ms. Carter and Ms. Christopher." The principal glanced at the note card in her hand. "They'll be doing a skit on our colonial settlers, followed by a folk dance."

The sight of his Sarah filing onto the stage with the other children nearly distracted him from Leigh's presence. He watched her glance from one child to another, obviously anxious to be sure she was doing it right. He caught the reassuring smile Leigh directed at her.

He knew from what Leigh had told him that he didn't have to worry during the skit. Sarah's role—a member of the crowd—was simple. Someone knelt to snap a picture. He should have thought to bring a camera, too. Sarah in her colonial bonnet was worth capturing.

The colonial leader muffed his lines, but nobody seemed to mind. There were indulgent smiles all around from the forgiving audience.

Then, too soon, it was time for the dance. He watched Leigh set the player carefully on the stage, saw her give a thumbs-up sign to the children. With some shuffling, some rearranging, they took their places. Sarah was between Meggie and a little girl with red curly hair. She glanced from one to the other, as if carefully measuring the distance between them.

Leigh held up her hand, nodded and pressed the button. Daniel held his breath, his palms clammy.

The children wove in and out in time to the music. He could see lips moving as they counted steps. Sarah, his little Sarah, went perfectly through the routine, eyes glued to the child in front of her. Probably nobody else in the room realized just how hard she was working. Nobody but Leigh, anyway.

The children did a complicated turn, and he heard a sigh of relief from Jamie when they all ended up going the right direction. It was almost over and—

The tape skipped. The twirling pattern of little figures wavered, uncertain, and the little redhead stumbled, bumping into Sarah, who careered into Meggie. Around the circle the pattern disintegrated.

The red-haired child grabbed Sarah's arm. "You dummy!" she shouted. "Look what you made me do! You're nothing but a dummy! I hate you!"

Chapter Fifteen

Leigh stumbled to her feet. She had to get to Sarah, had to comfort her, had to make her see it wasn't her fault. The rest of the kindergartners, confused, milled between her and Sarah.

"Emily, that is not the way my kindergartners behave." Amanda's voice left no room for doubt. "You may sit down."

Leigh hurried to Sarah and knelt beside her. "It's okay," she said, wiping the tears away. "It wasn't…"

Someone brushed against her, nearly knocking her over in his haste. Daniel. He snatched Sarah up in his arms, gave Leigh one furious, condemning look, and stalked out.

Leigh turned to Amanda, trying to keep the tears from her eyes.

"Go after him," Amanda said softly. "I'll take care of things here."

Leigh scrambled to her feet and hurried to the door. It still swung from Daniel's violent passage. Behind her, she could hear Amanda organizing the children for a bow over their nearly completed performance.

"Daniel!"

He was halfway to the door, and for an instant she thought he'd totally ignore her. Then he stopped and swung to face her, his expression bleak.

"Daniel, please don't." She reached toward him, thought the better of it, drew away her hand. "Please don't walk out like this. Let Sarah go back to the other children."

"Forget it." A muscle twitched angrily in his jaw. "I don't know how you can think I'd let her go back into that."

She touched Sarah gently. "I'm asking because it's best for Sarah."

"Best?" His voice rose. "How can you say that? You saw how those kids treated her!"

"I saw how one spoiled little girl reacted, and I'm sorry it happened." How could she make him understand? She could feel the pain, stronger than his anger, that radiated from him. "But you're not giving Sarah a chance to deal with it."

"I gave her a chance. I gave you a chance. It didn't work. Now I'm going to take care of my daughter my way."

Sarah's tears started again, and she buried her face in Daniel's shoulder.

Leigh took a shaky breath. She had to get him to see what he was doing. "Daniel, your anger is making it worse for her, don't you see that?"

"I see—" He stopped, then turned to look at Sarah. He wiped her tears away with gentle fingers. "Sarah, sugar, it's okay. Don't cry. Daddy's here."

"It's all right," Leigh said, touching Sarah's cheek

and then signing. "You didn't do anything wrong. Emily was just silly."

Daniel cradled Sarah against his shoulder, and Leigh could sense his struggle to control himself.

"Look…" He shook his head. "I know you were trying to do something good. I know you care about Sarah."

"I love Sarah." *And I love you.*

"But you were wrong." His voice, his expression, was uncompromising. "You were wrong. She's not ready for this, and probably she never will be."

"Daniel…" How could she argue with him when he was hurting so much?

"Just forget about it." He put his cheek against Sarah's. "Forget all this, and we can go back to where we were, Leigh."

Leigh stared at him, and she could read the message in his dark eyes plainly. Forget her plans for Sarah, her vision of what Sarah's life could be. Forget them, and maybe they could get back to where they had been, when there was some small chance of happiness between them.

All she had to do was say the words. But she couldn't. She knew that now. She could no more deny her dreams for Sarah than she could keep on denying the gift God had given her. She'd been trying that for months, and if there was one thing she'd learned from all this it was that denying your gifts didn't make them go away. It just made you unhappy.

She couldn't lie to Daniel, couldn't pretend she agreed with him, not even if it meant sacrificing everything there might have been between them.

"I can't." Her voice was soft. "Daniel, please try

to understand. I can't tell you something I don't believe.''

Daniel's expression was shuttered and locked
against her. ''Then we don't have anything to say to
each other.''

He turned and walked away.

''Leigh! Leigh, wake up.''

Leigh awoke from a dream of crying to discover
that her face was wet with tears. Jamie, silhouetted in
the light from the doorway, tactfully ignored them.

''Are you awake?''

Leigh pushed herself up to a sitting position. ''I'm
up.'' She glanced toward the window, to see only
darkness. ''What's going on? Is one of the kids
sick?''

''No, we're fine.''

But she could hear the tension in Jamie's voice.

''It's the weather.''

For an instant Leigh's mind was blank. The
weather? Then she remembered. ''The tropical
storm?''

''Hurricane now. Eleanor outsmarted all the fore-
casters. She regrouped, turned back into a hurricane.
And she's headed right for us.''

Leigh shot from the bed. ''How bad is it? How
soon?''

''Take it easy.'' Jamie squeezed her shoulder. ''I'd
forgotten you haven't been through this before. We
have some time. Maybe not as much as we should,
but we'll make it.''

''Are we going to evacuate?'' Leigh reached for
her jeans. ''Where's Josh?''

"Gone down to the marina to try to save the boats." Jamie's voice was grim.

"Heavens, I never thought of that." Leigh sent up a silent prayer, trying to imagine what saving the boats entailed. "What about evacuating?"

Jamie shrugged. "It's probably too late to get off the island. According to the radio, they'll stop the ferry after one more trip. But we wouldn't go anyway. I've got to get over to the elementary school and start setting up the shelter there."

She'd forgotten that was one of Jamie's many roles.

"I'll help you."

"I knew you would." Jamie turned to the door. "Just pack a small bag with things you'll need for one night. We'll give the kids some breakfast, then we'd better go. No rush, but I have a lot to do at the shelter."

Alone, Leigh pulled her clothes on, then stopped, arms half in her sweatshirt, to look out the window. Gray, nothing but gray. It wasn't even raining yet— she touched her face—except inside her.

Oh, Daniel.

What was he doing right now? Getting ready to meet the storm? Pulling out a duffel bag, as she was? Did he have a regretful thought to spare for her?

She should have seen it coming. Maybe she had seen it coming all along, but she'd refused to recognize it. She'd sensed from their first conversation that she and Daniel were going to be at odds over this issue. She just hadn't expected it to blow up in her face.

And she hadn't expected that, when the moment came, she'd be making a decision that would cost her a chance at happiness.

Your teaching ability is a God-given gift. Jamie had said that so many times, but she'd never really known what it meant. Not until she confronted it over Sarah and Daniel. Then she'd known. She couldn't turn her back on her gift. All her trying had been futile. She'd never find any peace that way.

Even now, in spite of the pain of knowing she'd lost Daniel for good, she couldn't say she'd have done anything differently. She just couldn't.

"Leigh? Are you ready?"

"Almost." She picked up her duffel bag. "I'll come help the kids."

When she got to the kitchen Mark and Meggie were at the table, cereal bowls in front of them, but they looked too excited to eat.

"The hurricane's coming, Auntie Leigh." Meggie's eyes were huge. "It's really coming."

Leigh touched her hair. "I know." If she hadn't been sure, the grave tones of the radio announcer would have convinced her. "We're going to be fine. It'll be an adventure."

"I should have gone with Daddy." Mark shoveled a spoonful of cereal in his mouth and talked around it. "I could have helped with the boats."

"Time enough for that when you're older," Jamie said, shoving a mug of coffee into Leigh's hand.

Leigh's eyes met her sister's, and she knew what Jamie was thinking. Hard enough to face having Josh out in that, without worrying about Mark, too.

"Will Josh come to the shelter after he sees about the boats?" she asked, soft voiced.

"Probably not." Jamie tried on a smile that didn't quite work. "He'll find plenty to do at the marina."

"But you and the kids…"

"We all have our jobs to do. He took the cell phone, so he'll try to stay in touch if he can."

A spatter of rain hissed against the window, startling Leigh. She looked out, to see the palmettos begin to dance with the wind. It was starting.

"Do you think..." She hesitated, swallowed hard and tried again. "Do you think Daniel and Sarah will come to the shelter?"

Jamie shook her head, her eyes filled with sympathetic pain. "I doubt it. He never has before. Anyway, that place of his has withstood a lot of years of storms. They'll probably just stay put."

"I wish Sarah would come to the shelter." Meggie slid off her chair. "I want to take my paper dolls, in case she comes. Then we can play."

"Good idea. I'm sure you'll find someone to play paper dolls with." Jamie rinsed bowls and set them in the sink. "Now, let's finish getting our bags packed. One small bag, remember. That's the rule."

Leigh helped Meggie, which was no easy task. Meggie wanted to take everything she owned, but constant repetition of the rule finally convinced her. When they returned to the kitchen, Jamie handed Leigh a yellow slicker.

"You'll need this. And I thought we'd better take two cars, just in case."

In case of what, Leigh wanted to ask. Then she decided she'd rather not know. "Fine. Who wants to ride with me?"

"Me, me!" Meggie bounced up and down. "I'll go with Auntie Leigh."

Mark nodded gravely. "I'll take care of Mommy." He picked up his bag. "I'm ready to go."

Leigh stepped outside. And into a downpour. The

rain spilled from the sky, thundered on the roof, splashed from gutters and sent a fine mist rising from the road. It took her breath away, freezing her for a moment.

She grabbed Meggie's hand. "Let's run for it!"

They got in the car, and she switched on the radio. She was beginning to understand the constant compulsion islanders had to have the weather station on. Even if you couldn't do anything about it, you wanted to know.

The rain streamed down the windshield, and she switched on lights and wipers. This was not going to be a fun drive.

Be with us, Lord. Somehow this didn't seem the time for a more involved prayer than that. In an emergency, the simplest petitions were enough, like a child calling "Help me" to a loving parent.

Meggie bounced in spite of the restraint of her seat belt. She didn't, thank goodness, have any idea how serious this was.

"I hope Sarah comes to the shelter. This will be fun. It's like going camping."

"I guess it is."

Meggie seemed to think the hurricane had been arranged for her amusement, but probably that was better than being terrified.

"Mommy has a lot to do to get ready for people, so you need to help, you know."

"I can be a big help." Meggie wiggled again. "Auntie Leigh, why's this in the seat?"

Leigh glanced at the object Meggie pulled out of the seat crevice, and her heart seemed to stop.

"It's a shell." The shell Daniel and Sarah had given her that night on the beach...the night Daniel kissed her, the night the air between them had been filled with possibilities.

"It's a whelk," Meggie said knowledgeably. She put the shell in Leigh's hand. "Did you lose it?"

Leigh's fingers curled around the shell. It was rough and forbidding on the outside, intricately beautiful inside. Like Daniel.

Her heart wasn't stopped anymore. Nothing that was stopped could possibly hurt this much.

"Yes, I guess I did lose it." She'd lost a lot more than just a shell.

She took a deep breath, fingers tightening on the shell, its rough surface biting into her skin. She'd lost. Or had she given up too easily? Daniel, presenting that forbidding face to her... But had she really done her best to convince him?

She'd been trying all summer to run away, trying to convince herself that was the sensible thing to do. It hadn't worked with her job. Maybe it wasn't meant to work with Daniel, either.

"Zip up your slicker, Meggie." Leigh slowed, flicked her lights at Jamie's car and hit the horn. "I'm going to put you in Mommy's car. I have to do something."

Stopping the car behind Jamie's, she put the flashers on and slid out, then hurried Meggie through the rain to the other car.

"I'm going back." She had to shout over the rain pounding on the roof. "I've got to go check on Daniel and Sarah."

"But Leigh..."

"I've got to." She closed the door on Jamie's objections.

She ran back to her car, slid in and slammed the

door. She had to go back. The idea gripped her mind. She couldn't give up this easily. Not with her happiness and Sarah's and Daniel's at stake.

Turning the car around required concentration. Biting her lip, she maneuvered cautiously. If she veered off to the side, she'd slide into the mud-brown ditch in an instant.

Finally reversed, Leigh headed back down the road. She'd go past Jamie's, then onto the main road that ran along the ocean, and pray she could get through.

The rain went from pouring to pounding, so loud on the roof of the car that she could barely hear the radio. She turned up the volume, trying to drown it out.

And wished she hadn't. None of the news was good. The ferry couldn't get through; nothing could. Everyone on the island would be there for the duration. Eleanor, packing winds of over 120 miles an hour and fifteen-foot waves, had drawn a bead directly on them. Worse, it looked as if the storm's eye wall would hit at high tide.

The gravity in the announcer's voice made it clear that was bad, and Leigh suspected she didn't want to know just how bad. Clenching the wheel a bit tighter, she aimed the car toward Daniel's and prayed.

Chapter Sixteen

Wind snatched the board from Daniel's grip, tossing it aside like a piece of tissue paper. He reached for another, struggling to keep it close to his body as he balanced on the second story of the construction. A gust sent a spray of water down his neck, but he was already so wet it didn't matter.

He glanced out to sea, then almost wished he hadn't. Gray-black clouds roiled ominously nearer, whipping the heavy waves into a frenzy. The wind howled around the construction site like something demented. It would get worse before it got better, a lot worse, from the look of it. And he was alone.

If they'd realized last night, Joe would have stayed. Instead, convinced Eleanor would blow out to sea, Daniel had sent Joe off to his daughter's birthday party, in spite of the old man's reluctance. He should have listened, should have paid attention to someone's opinion besides his own.

Should have. He managed to wedge the board against the uprights. Should have, if only. None of those did any good. If he'd listened to Joe, Sarah wouldn't be alone up in the house while he battled the storm. If Leigh were there...

He shut his mind to that thought, slammed the door on the treacherous weakness that came with it. It was over with Leigh. He'd known from the beginning that he couldn't rely on anyone else, and she'd proved him right. She'd let Sarah get hurt; she'd refused to admit she was wrong; she'd—

Whoa, back off. He wasn't going to think about that anymore, remember? Not now, anyway.

Now he had to ignore the gnawing pain in his gut and get the job done. Get the wall braced. Get back to Sarah before the storm got any worse. Poor kid, she was probably scared silly. At least she couldn't hear the wind.

He hammered the last nail in place, took a step back, struggling to keep his balance against the wind that threatened to flatten him. That should do it. As long as it didn't get too much worse...

As if the wind heard, it blasted against him, throwing a sheet of water into his face, into his eyes, blurring his vision. He blinked, dashed the water away with his hand, looked up.

The wall above him wavered, creaked in protest like a child crying out. He reached toward it, shouting some inarticulate protest. And saw the beam coming straight at him.

By the time she'd nearly reached Jamie's house, Leigh's fingers were cramped on the wheel and sweat slicked her face. Driving in this was impossible. If she had to listen to the thunder of rain on the car roof for one more moment, she thought she'd go mad.

She bit her lip, narrowing her eyes to peer down the road toward Daniel's. Wind whipped the rain sideways, and branches flew from the trees as though slapped by a giant hand. The power lines danced and swayed.

Stop at Jamie's, the voice of reason murmured. *Stop and call. At least try to be sure they're at the house before you go any farther.*

If she could get through on the phone, if the lines hadn't gone down...well, she wouldn't lose more than a few minutes by trying. She slid into Jamie's driveway, slammed on the brake and ran for the house.

She banged the door closed and leaned against it, gasping for breath. The relative silence was an almost physical relief. The wind still howled and the rain still hammered, but they were muted now by walls and roof.

Leigh shivered, thinking of Josh out in this, struggling with the other fishermen to save the boats. *Oh, Lord, Your sea is so wide, and my boat is so small.* Half-forgotten words shivered through her mind with a lonely echo.

What was Josh doing? Her mind ran up against a blank wall of ignorance. She had no idea, but she suspected it was dangerous, and her lips moved in prayer as she crossed toward the phone.

Now, if only the phone still worked...

Even as she had the thought, it rang. Leigh ran to it, snatched it up. Josh, calling to see if they'd gotten out?

"Hello?"

The line hummed emptily in her ear.

"Hello?" she said, louder.

Nothing. Maybe it was a mistake.

She started to put it down, when a frightened voice sounded.

"Leigh? Leigh?"

Her heart stopped, then slammed against her ribs. It was Sarah.

"Sarah!" She shouted the word into the receiver. "It's Leigh, honey. Are you okay?"

She knew Sarah wouldn't be able to make out the words, but maybe she'd catch some sound, at least know she'd gotten through. *Please, God.*

A moment of silence, a moment when she almost thought she'd imagined hearing Sarah.

"Daddy." Sarah's voice choked with tears. "Daddy's hurt. Help."

The phone went dead.

Oh, Lord, please. The rest of the words didn't want to form. Maybe it didn't matter. Now, of all times, God knew the prayer her heart cried.

She rattled the connection on the phone, knowing it was useless but compelled to try anyway. Nothing. No way of contacting anyone else. No way of letting anyone else know Daniel was hurt and Sarah...

Sarah must be alone. If Joe had been there, he'd have called.

Leigh's heart clenched. Daniel hurt, Sarah alone. She had to get to them.

She ran to the door, then stopped, blood pounding in her ears, mind whirling. *Think.* Josh might come back. If he did, she had to let him know what was happening.

She raced back to the phone, scribbled a message on the pad, then propped it up. That was all she could do, that and pray.

Clenching the soggy slicker around her, she forced the door open.

Lightning glittered, dashing wickedly toward the earth. The wind caught her breath, the rain slammed against her. She lowered her head and battled toward the car.

Careful, careful. She pulled back out of the driveway. One wrong turn of the wheel would sent her into the deep ditch that roared with water. She couldn't fail, not now, not with Daniel and Sarah depending on her.

Just a couple of miles—that's all it was. She could do this. She could see only a few feet beyond her headlights, but that would be enough. God would light just enough of the path to keep her going.

Wind battered the car, and it shivered under the onslaught. Water poured across the windshield faster than the wipers could work, blinding her.

The wipers cleared her vision for an instant, and she hit the brake, shuddering. Ahead of her, a downed power line writhed and sparked like a fiery snake across the road.

She took a deep breath, uttered an incoherent prayer and barreled past it. The sparks painted afterimages on her vision and the acrid scent of ozone filled the car, but she was through.

Not long, not long now. She was going to make it. She had to. Daniel, Sarah. *Oh, Lord, protect them.*

Pain. Pain in his head. Daniel groped, exploring, and discovered a lump the size of a turtle's egg on his forehead. No wonder it hurt. Whatever had hit him must have affected his hearing, too. The roaring in his ears deafened...

Then he knew where he was. That wasn't his hearing. That was Hurricane Eleanor, doing her best to blow him and his precious building right off the island.

He opened his eyes, struggled to focus and muttered. The wall he'd spent the last week building had come down smack on top of him. He blinked, trying to assess the damage. A timber pinned his left arm, another his legs.

He flexed his legs, encountered more pain, took a breath and tried again. He had to get out, had to get to Sarah.

The heavy timber didn't move. He shoved against it, setting his teeth into his lip. Blast, the thing wouldn't budge. With his arm and his legs pinned he couldn't get any leverage. Might as well try to lift a house with one finger.

He sank back against the rough planks, exhausted. Wind drove the rain into his face. It stung like somebody slapping him, telling him he couldn't give up. Telling him he had to keep trying, had to get free for Sarah's sake. She was all alone.

A fresh gust hit the building, and the timbers beneath him screamed in protest. No good. It was no good. He couldn't get out, couldn't do a thing to save himself. He was helpless, as helpless as a baby, and there was no one in the world who knew or cared.

He put a hand to his face. Rain and salt tears mixed. Sarah was alone in the house. What was she thinking? That he'd gone away and left her, just as her mother had? He'd promised to protect her, and look what kind of job he'd done.

And Leigh...where was she? Safe, please let her be safe.

Pain gripped his heart, blacker than the storm. He'd let down everyone he'd ever loved. He'd been so sure he could handle things himself, so sure he didn't need anyone. Now look at the result.

Slowly, words forced themselves through the pain. *God, if You're there, if You can even listen to me any more, help Sarah. Protect her. I can't. I can't do it by myself. Help me.*

The wind roared, battering his senses, deafening him. The building swayed under him, fighting the wind. This was it, the last thing he'd hear—

"Daniel! Daniel!"

He squirmed, turning his head, squinting through the gray downpour toward an incredible circle of yellow light.

"Daniel." She scrambled toward him. It was Leigh, yellow beam dancing from a flashlight in her hand. "Are you hurt? How bad is it?"

She dropped to her knees next to him, hands reaching. He grabbed her hand, held on tight, feeling warm skin, fine bones. Leigh. It really was Leigh.

"How did you get here?" Then he remembered. "Sarah...never mind me, go to Sarah."

"Sarah's fine." Leigh had to shout against the wind. She pulled at the timber that pinned him, straining to move it. "She called me."

Called? That didn't make sense, but there wasn't time to think about it now.

"You'll have to get something to use as a lever. We'll never move it without help."

Leigh nodded, and at the movement the wind whipped her hood back. Her hair, soaked, clung to her head, and her eyes were huge, frightened, determined.

She turned and scrabbled across the floor on all fours, swinging the light. It hit a loose two-by-four. She grabbed the end of it and dragged it back to him.

"Will this work?"

"It should." The wind forced the words back down his throat. "Wedge it under the timber. Then you'll need a fulcrum."

Leigh worked the two-by-four in place, then shoved his toolbox under it.

"Ready?" She stood, staggered against the wind, steadied herself.

He nodded, bracing his free hand against the timber and gritting his teeth. "Do it."

She pulled, putting her whole weight into it. The timber groaned and protested. His muscles strained against the weight. Finally the timber shifted, lifted. His arm was free.

"Your arm." Leigh shoved the timber aside and dropped to her knees next to him. "Is it broken?"

"It's fine." He flexed his fist, then sat up, reaching for the timber that pinned his legs. Leigh pushed; he pushed. It slid slowly off him.

He swung onto his knees, suppressed a groan. Hurt, but nothing seemed to be broken.

"Okay." He grabbed Leigh's arm for support, struggled to his feet. "Let's get out of here before the whole thing goes."

Arms around each other, they staggered toward safety.

Chapter Seventeen

Leigh clutched Daniel's arm as they struggled toward the house, incoherent thank-yous bubbling through her mind. *Thank You, Lord. Thank You.* He was safe. Sarah was safe. That was all that mattered.

Even as she thought it, Leigh knew that wasn't all that mattered to her. With Daniel's arm strong around her as they fought the wind, she could almost believe the differences between them were resolved.

Almost, but not quite. Probably he'd have been equally glad to see anyone who arrived to help him. The fact that it was she—given how reluctant he was to rely on her, this might make matters even worse between them.

They lurched up the few steps to the porch, fighting the wind that buffeted them. Daniel forced open the door. They spilled inside, the door slamming behind them.

Peace—relative peace, anyway. Her ears rang with the quiet, as if the storm were still there, inside her head. She straightened. They were here; they were safe. She'd begun to fear they'd both die out there, but God had brought them through the storm.

Then she realized that Daniel's arms were still around her.

She looked up. His lean wet face, inches from hers, was indescribably dear to her. *Safe,* her mind echoed, and for the first time since she'd heard Sarah's voice on the phone, she could take a breath without pain clutching her heart.

The lines in his face smoothed slowly, and his arms tightened around her. Her heart stuttered, thudding in her ears, and she pressed against him. His eyes darkened; his mouth neared hers—

"Daddy!" Sarah raced at them full tilt, arms outstretched.

In an instant Daniel released Leigh and scooped up his daughter in his arms.

"It's okay, sweetheart. We're all okay." His cheek pressed against hers. "We're safe now."

Leigh's legs decided not to hold her up any longer, and she slumped into a chair. She ought to get rid of the soggy slicker, but even breathing seemed too much effort.

"I'm getting you all wet, honey." Daniel put Sarah down. She scampered after the kitten, which was investigating Leigh's soggy shoes.

Daniel slid out of his slicker, shook it, then draped it over one of the kitchen chairs. He pulled the clammy knit shirt away from his body and looked at Leigh. "We'd better get dried off, both of us, before we catch pneumonia."

"Shouldn't we try to make it to the shelter before it gets any worse?" Leigh glanced toward the window, but she couldn't see anything beyond the tape except gray, driving rain.

Daniel shook his head, droplets spraying from his wet hair. "I think we're past that point already. It's safer to stay here than to go out on the roads."

Stay here? Together? Leigh opened her mouth to protest, then closed it.

Daniel probably knew far more about hurricanes than she did. In fact, the radio on the countertop seemed to be broadcasting the same message. "Power lines and trees down all over the island, and the worst of it is yet to come. Residents are urged to stay off the roads if at all possible. Updates..."

"The worst is yet to come?" She hoped her voice didn't waver.

Daniel gave her a rueful smile. "Afraid so. Don't worry. This old house stood through Hugo. It can withstand worse than Eleanor's going to throw at us. I promise."

He pulled a dish towel off the rack and tossed it at her. She caught it, wiped wet face, wet hair.

"So I guess we're here for the duration." She tried for a smile she didn't feel.

"I guess so." His eyes lingered on her face, as if he wanted to say something and didn't know how. Then his expression changed and he glanced at Sarah. "How did you get here, anyway? Isn't Jamie in charge of the shelter? I thought you'd be with her."

"We were headed there when..." She hesitated, editing her words. "I went back to the house for something. I didn't expect it to get so bad so fast." She shuddered. "I've never been through a hurricane before, remember?"

"Nobody expected it to get this bad. If I had, I sure

wouldn't have chased Joe off to his daughter's last night.'' Daniel's expression turned somber. ''I wouldn't have risked leaving Sarah here alone.''

Again she had the impression that he held something back, as if he wrestled with something he wasn't ready to talk about yet.

''So Joe's safe.''

He nodded. ''Should be. His daughter lives over on Forest Road. That's well away from any trouble spots.'' He frowned. ''But you didn't answer my question. Why did you come here?''

Leigh's heart thumped, and her fingers closed over the shell in her pocket. She couldn't. She couldn't, just like that, blurt out the real reason she'd turned back.

''I told you. Sarah called me.''

He blinked, looked from her to Sarah. ''Sarah called you? On the phone?''

''On the phone.'' Now she could smile. ''She dialed the number—she got through—she told me you were hurt.''

''But how?'' He stopped, looking dumbfounded. ''How could she possibly do that? I never dreamed…'' He shook his head. ''And how did she know? How did she know I was trapped?''

Leigh turned to Sarah. ''Sarah, how did you know about Daddy? That Daddy was hurt?''

Sarah pointed to the corner of the kitchen. There, on the floor, lay a child-sized slicker and a pair of small, wet boots.

''I saw,'' Sarah signed.

''She went out in that…'' Daniel stopped, sank onto the chair, held his arms out to Sarah. She stepped into them, and he pulled her close.

For a long moment he was silent, his cheek pressed to Sarah's dark hair. Then he looked up at Leigh.

"I never dreamed she'd go out after me. She must have seen, realized she couldn't get me out by herself, come back and called. She…" His arms tightened around his daughter, his voice going husky. "She's quite a girl, isn't she?"

Leigh's heart seemed to be singing, though her eyes filled with tears. "I don't think you could expect most five-year-olds to do that. Hearing or not." She touched Sarah's shoulder. "Good job, Sarah. Good job."

Sarah smiled, then slid down from her father's lap. The kitten pounced on her shoelaces, and she giggled. Just like any five-year-old.

"Well." Daniel cleared his throat. "As I said, we'd better get changed. Sorry I can't offer you a hot shower, but the power's gone off."

Leigh made a gigantic effort and struggled out of the slicker. "Just being dry will feel like heaven."

"I know what you mean. Look, raid my room. You ought to find something that'll work for you. At least it'll be dry." He ruffled Sarah's hair. "My daughter and I will finish the hurricane preparation together."

The pride on his face when he gazed at Sarah told Leigh he saw her in a whole new way. Tears stung Leigh's eyes again. Sarah had taken her future into her own small hands.

Once upstairs, she opened the door to Daniel's room hesitantly. Neat, spare, masculine— If Ashley had once made an impact on this room, her presence had been wiped out by now. She visualized Daniel stripping the room of every sign of Ashley's presence, and she winced. If he'd been that pained by her defection...

She put that thought away and headed for the dresser. Get dry—get dressed—go downstairs and help. A wind-borne branch slammed against the side of the house, emphasizing the thought. They weren't out of danger yet. This was no time to be mooning over what might have been between her and Daniel. If he was ready to change his mind about Sarah's future, that was success enough.

When she got back downstairs, Daniel was lighting the kerosene lamps Joe had gotten ready. He looked up at her, wet hair spilling onto his forehead. "All dry?"

Maybe it was her imagination that his eyes lingered on her face. "Much better." She reached for the matches. "Now you go and change. I can do this."

He put the matchbox in her hand, his closing over hers, and her skin warmed at the touch.

"Right you are."

He released her, went from the room, and she could breathe again.

She turned to Sarah. "Where shall we put this one? In the living room?"

Sarah nodded, and Leigh carefully carried the lamp into the adjoining room. This was going to be difficult, very difficult. The three of them, marooned here together against the power of the storm—it would be too easy to let herself feel as if they were a family. Easy, and ultimately painful.

By the time they had all the lamps placed, Daniel had come back down.

"Very cheerful." He nodded approvingly. "I'll get

the heater ready to go, too. It'll get a lot chillier in here before it's over.''

A crack sounded from outdoors, and Leigh's gaze flew to the window. She swallowed hard, trying to ignore the sick feeling in her stomach. "How long do you think it will last?"

He shrugged. "Depends on the storm track and speed. Several hours, at least. Maybe longer." He switched on the radio in the living room. "Guess we'd better keep this on, just in case."

In case of what, she wanted to ask. Or maybe she didn't. How he could be so calm was beyond her.

"Come on."

Daniel gripped her shoulder, seeming to guess what she felt.

"We're going to be okay. Let Eleanor do her worst. We can take it."

Leigh bit her lip. "And the others? Josh, and the other fishermen? And Jamie?"

"They've all been through it before." His eyes darkened. "I won't lie to you, Leigh. It's dangerous. But they know what to do."

She looked up at him, feeling the grip of his hand anchoring her. "I'd like to pray for their safety. Will you join me?"

She expected a refusal, or at least an evasion. But instead he nodded.

"Sounds like the right idea." He held out his hand to Sarah. "Come on, sweetheart. We're going to pray."

The three of them held hands, and Leigh blinked back sudden tears.

"Dear Lord…"

Her voice gained strength as she spoke, asking

God's protection for all those who fought the storm's fury. A current seemed to run from her hand to Sarah's to Daniel's as they prayed, as if they were connected by the living Spirit. Her fear ebbed, and warmth blossomed inside her.

"Amen," she said.

"Amen," Daniel echoed.

A few hours later, Daniel wondered if his reassurances had been too hasty. Eleanor might end up being even worse than Hurricane Hugo had been. At least Hugo hadn't hit the island head on.

He sipped at the cocoa Leigh had made on the kerosene heater and watched Leigh and Sarah, sitting on cushions on the living-room floor with a game. The kitten pounced on a piece as Sarah moved it, earning a giggle, and the lanterns made Leigh's hair glow like gold.

Ridiculous, to be thinking how cozy they all were, here together, when the storm worsened by the moment. Just because Leigh was with them... He wanted to back away from that thought, but he couldn't. What was she thinking behind that brave smile? Had she come back only for Sarah, or was there still a chance for him?

Unanswerable questions, at least for now. He reached out to turn up the radio.

Nothing but bad news, far as he could tell. They were completely isolated, cut off from any kind of help. The storm had taken dead aim at the island, packing winds of 130 miles an hour. All anyone could do was dig in and ride it out.

The crack of another tree splintering interrupted the steady howl of the wind, and the old house creaked as if in sympathy. He glanced at Leigh, saw her green eyes widen. But the hand that moved a counter in the game never wavered.

"Four, five spaces." She handed the spinner to Sarah. "Your turn."

"Who's winning?"

She looked up at him, managing a smile that had just the faintest shadow of apprehension behind it. "Sarah is, so far. But I'll beat her yet."

Sarah giggled again and moved her marker across the finish line with an air of triumph.

"You won again!" Leigh clapped. "Good going, Sarah. You're the champion."

"She really is, isn't she? A champion."

Leigh's smile lit her face. "Isn't that what I've been telling you?"

"Yes, you have. Always. I guess I wasn't ready to hear it. Especially not after what happened at the school." He paused, his voice roughening. "And then you were gone, and I thought you weren't coming back."

She glanced down suddenly, and he thought her cheeks got a little pinker. "About that—there's something I wanted to say to you."

He leaned forward. She was close enough to touch, but he resisted the temptation. "What?"

"What I told you about coming here today—that wasn't all."

His eyebrows lifted. "What's the rest of it?"

She took a breath. "I'd already started back when I got Sarah's call. I was coming anyway."

He stood on the edge of a precipice, afraid to move a foot because it might be the wrong step. "Why were you coming, Leigh?'' Why, with a hurricane threatening, were you coming here?

Her eyes slid away from his. "I just kept going over and over what happened, and I couldn't leave it alone. I couldn't just give up on you. And Sarah.''

"Sarah.''

"Yes.'' She leaned toward him, eyes meeting his again. "Daniel, surely this has convinced you. Sarah... Sarah doesn't need to be coddled and treated like a baby. And she certainly doesn't need to be sent away to school. She can learn to handle the Emilys of this world. She can go to school right here, with you.''

Sarah moved and caught his eye. Frowning, she seemed to be following some of what Leigh was saying in spite of the fact that Leigh wasn't signing. Suddenly she smiled and pounced onto the game board.

"Sarah, school,'' she said proudly. She pointed to herself. "School.''

Daniel swallowed a lump the size of a boulder in his throat. Maybe his little girl was braver than he was. He looked at Leigh. "I still want to protect her. I don't want to let her go.''

Leigh shook her head. "It's not letting her go, Daniel,'' she said softly. "It's letting her grow.''

The quiet words echoed in his mind. He held out his hand to Sarah, and she grabbed it and swung on it.

"I guess you're right,'' he said. "Besides, I couldn't possibly get along without her now.''

Sarah slept, the kitten curled beside her. Leigh tucked the afghan over them gently.

"She's fine." Daniel moved a little, making room beside him on the couch. "Come and sit, Leigh."

She sat down cautiously, very aware of him. Sarah slept; the kitten slept; the storm raged outside. They were alone in a warm cocoon of safety.

"It's getting worse, isn't it?" She glanced toward the taped window. Even on the sheltered side of the house, a maelstrom whirled. She didn't need the radio announcer to tell her that.

Daniel put his hand over hers where it lay between them on the fabric. The warm reassurance of his grasp flowed into her.

"The eye wall is almost here. That'll be the worst." His grip tightened. "We're going to be okay. I know."

The conviction in his voice almost convinced her. "I hope you're right." She managed a shaky smile. "I really don't want to be out in this again."

"You won't be. Not until it's over."

A shadow crossed his face. Was he thinking about those moments when he'd been trapped?

"How is your arm?" She touched it lightly. "And your legs? You probably ought to see a doctor when this is over."

He shrugged off that idea impatiently. "I'm fine. There were a couple of moments when I thought I wouldn't be, but I'm fine."

"When I saw you there..." Remembered fear gripped her, and her hand tightened on his. "I was so scared."

He lifted their clasped hands. "Me, too." He paused, staring at their hands for a long moment. "Maybe that was just what I needed."

Her eyes met his. "I don't..."

He put her hand to his lips, and she lost the rest of whatever she'd been going to say.

"I thought I could do it all myself." His voice grew husky. "I thought I didn't need God, didn't need anyone. I was wrong." His lips brushed her fingers, gentle as a prayer. "When I knew I couldn't help myself, I cried out to God."

Joy bubbled up in Leigh. "And God answered."

He smiled. "God sent me peace. And then He sent me you."

"I'm so glad." The words were inadequate to express the singing in her heart.

He looked up suddenly. "Listen."

"The quiet!" Leigh's breath caught. "Is it over?"

"No." He put his arm around her, drawing her close against him. "We're in the eye of the storm, sweetheart. The still center." He put their clasped hands against his chest, and she could feel the steady beat of his heart.

"How long?"

"Only a few minutes, probably. Then the other side of the eye wall will hit." His arm tightened around her. "But we'll be okay."

"I know." The peace that flooded her wouldn't allow any other answer.

His look touched her like a caress, and then his hand stroked her cheek. "I love you, Leigh. I think I started loving you that first day when I saw you with Sarah. I've done everything I could think of to keep it from happening, and none of it did any good. I think I was meant to love you."

"Daniel..." His lips cut off her words. She touched his face, drawing him nearer, falling headlong into the magic of his kiss.

"I love you, Daniel," she murmured against his mouth. "I love you."

The old house shook as the full fury of the storm hit it again. In the circle of Daniel's arms, Leigh was safe.

Chapter Eighteen

"Daniel! Leigh!"

The loud voice, accompanied by even louder knocking, roused Leigh. She sat up, half-awake, realizing she'd been sound asleep against Daniel's shoulder.

He straightened, smiling, and rubbed his arm where her head had rested. "It's about time, sleepyhead. Sounds like Josh is here."

Leigh ran to the door, flinging it open, letting in the gray light of early dawn.

"Josh!" She threw herself into his arms and hugged him fiercely. "You're all right! What about Jamie and the kids?"

"Everyone's fine." Josh hugged her back, then disentangled himself to slap Daniel's shoulder. "Man, I'm glad to see the two of you. Thought maybe you got blown out into the Gulf Stream."

"This old place wouldn't give in to a little blow like Eleanor," Daniel said easily, as if the hurricane had been a minor blip. Then his face sobered. "What's the news? How bad is it?"

"No deaths," Josh said quickly. "Far as we can tell, anyway. But a lot of damage."

"The boats?" Daniel asked.

"We saved most of them, except for those few at Juniper Point. They broke up on the rocks." He shook his head. "We're going to be a long time cleaning up and getting over this. Still, it could have been a lot worse."

"Where do you need the most help?"

"Shelter's full." Josh glanced at Leigh. "Jamie could use some help there. And we're still checking the houses down at South Beach."

"I'll go right away." Leigh's mind reeled with all that had to be done. No deaths, she reminded herself. They could deal with the rest of it. Jamie would know what to do.

Daniel put his arm around Leigh. "We'll both be out to help, soon as we can get ready. You want something to eat?"

"I had breakfast at the shelter when I stopped to check on Jamie and the kids." He grinned. "Meggie says to bring Sarah to the shelter. Most of the kindergartners are there, and they want to play with her."

"Will do," Daniel said easily, as if he'd never doubted the wisdom of that.

Josh turned away, and Leigh grabbed him and kissed his cheek.

"Thank God we all came through it," she murmured.

"Amen." He patted her cheek. "Got to go. I'll catch you later."

The door closed. Sarah stumbled toward them,

clutching the kitten. She yawned, and Daniel ruffled her hair.

"Why don't you two get something to eat," he said. "I want to go down to the site and check on how the construction came through."

Leigh caught his arm. "We'll all go."

He looked for a moment as though he'd give her an argument, and then he nodded. "All right. We'll all go."

The path was a tangle of downed trees, bits of lumber, trailing palmetto fronds. Leigh picked her way carefully in Daniel's wake, and he carried Sarah.

Apprehension tied her stomach in knots. What were they going to find? Daniel had been right about the old house's ability to withstand the storm, but what about the new construction?

They emerged from the trees into the open, and Daniel set Sarah down. The ocean, gray and angry, still roared, but the sky stretched crystal blue and cloudless, as if the storm had never been. Sandpipers chased one another along the line of wet sand, and gulls stood facing the wind.

Leigh forced herself to turn and look at the construction.

No. At what was left of the construction. Clutching Sarah's hand, she followed Daniel to the remains of his dream.

Eleanor had done a good job. Where two stories had been nearly completed, only a tumble of lumber, like a child's game of jackstraws, remained.

Leigh tried to swallow over the lump in her throat. She drew Sarah a little closer against her side. Gone, everything was gone except the foundation. All Daniel's hard work...

She looked at him, trying to read the expression in his dark eyes as he studied the destruction of his dream. Her heart hurt for him, and mixed with the pain was fear. His renewed faith was so fragile. Could it stand a blow like this?

She felt a stab of pain, maybe even fear. This could so easily send him back into his shell, back into believing he couldn't rely on God or anyone else.

She couldn't say anything. She didn't have the words that would make this all right. She could only wait.

"Well." He turned to them, managed a smile. "Looks like I've got some rebuilding to do."

Leigh found she could breathe again. She touched his arm. "Daniel, I'm so sorry."

He reached for her, pulling her into the circle of his arms and then lifting Sarah to join them. "I thought about this a lot last night, about how I'd feel if it was all gone." He shook his head, smiling. "And you know what? It doesn't matter. All that matters is right here."

His arms tightened around them. "The rest can be replaced. I can't replace the two of you. I can't replace my family."

Family. Leigh gave herself up to the joy that flooded through her. All that really mattered was that, with God's blessing, they were a family.

She'd found the life God had intended for her all along. They all had. God had given the three of them more than they'd dreamed of asking. Hugging Sarah, Leigh lifted her face for Daniel's kiss.

Epilogue

Daniel stood on the veranda of the lodge addition, watching his wife and daughter.

Leigh and Sarah sat at the picnic table under the trees, painting with Meggie, Mark and three of the children whose parents had checked in yesterday. He walked across to them, stopping behind Leigh and resting his hands lightly on her shoulders. She glanced up at him with a quick, loving smile.

Leigh had been right about the picnic tables under the trees, and the rocking chairs on the veranda. She'd made all the decorating decisions when the addition was finally finished.

Had it only been two years since the hurricane? In the wake of the devastation, it had seemed to some islanders they'd never recover. They hadn't reckoned on the outpouring of support. Help had flooded the island, most of it from churches across the country. Not just money or food or clothing, though they'd needed that. It was the people Daniel would never forget, like the team from a church somewhere in

Pennsylvania that had just turned up, tools in hand, to help him rebuild.

Daniel's hand tightened on his wife's shoulders, thinking of those volunteers whose names he'd never known. *God's love in action,* Leigh had called it. Maybe that experience with outsiders had helped to smooth the island's transition when the bridge was finally finished and they were linked, permanently, with the mainland.

"Good job, Sarah." Leigh touched Sarah's painting.

Sarah smiled, adding another seagull to a bright blue sky. She'd blossomed so much in her two years at the island school with Leigh serving as her translator and a part-time teacher. Sometimes it was hard to remember the solemn little creature she'd once been.

"That is nice, Sarah." He signed as he spoke, but Sarah lip-read so well that sometimes it seemed they hardly needed to sign. "Yours, too, Meggie."

Meggie leaned across to scrutinize Sarah's picture, then nodded. "I like it."

Sarah's smile flashed. "Sarah," she pointed with her paintbrush to the figures she'd drawn. "Daddy. Mommy."

Leigh's hand came up to cover his. The first time Sarah had called her "Mommy," her tears had spilled over. He knew it still had the power to move her.

"What's this?" He touched the blue object next to Leigh in the picture.

Sarah's eyes widened. "Baby," she said firmly. "Brother," she added.

"That's right, Sarah." He put his hand on his wife's expanding waist and felt the tiny flutter of a kick. Leigh leaned back against him, smiling. He dropped a light kiss on her lips.

"Family," Leigh said softly.

His eyes were suddenly wet with gratitude. Family. God had indeed given him far more than he could ever have asked or imagined.

* * * * *

Dear Reader,

Thank you for reading my Love Inspired® novel,
A Father's Promise. I hope that you enjoyed the story
of Daniel and Leigh, two people stubbornly headed
away from God's will, but brought together by a special
little girl. May it touch your heart as it touched mine
while I wrote it.

God always gives us more than we could possibly
imagine. As Leigh and Daniel discovered that in my
story, I hope you've discovered that in your life.

Best Wishes,

Marta Perry

Take 3 inspirational love stories FREE!

PLUS get a FREE surprise gift!

Special Limited-time Offer

Mail to Steeple Hill Reader Service™
3010 Walden Avenue
P.O. Box 1867
Buffalo, N.Y. 14240-1867

YES! Please send me 3 free Love Inspired™ novels and my free surprise gift. Then send me 3 brand-new novels every month, which I will receive months before they appear in bookstores. Bill me at the low price of $3.19 each plus 25¢ delivery and applicable sales tax, if any*. That's the complete price and a saving of over 10% off the cover prices—quite a bargain! I understand that accepting the books and gift places me under no obligation ever to buy any books. I can always return a shipment and cancel at any time. Even if I never buy another book from Steeple Hill, the 3 free books and the surprise gift are mine to keep forever.

103 IEN CFAG

Name	(PLEASE PRINT)	
Address		Apt. No.
City	State	Zip

This offer is limited to one order per household and not valid to present Love Inspired™ subscribers. *Terms and prices are subject to change without notice. Sales tax applicable in New York.

ULI-198   ©1997 Steeple Hill

Harlequin Romance®

Invites You to A Wedding!

Whirlwind Weddings
Combines the heady romance of a whirlwind courtship with the excitement of a wedding—strong heroes, feisty heroines and marriages made not so much in heaven as in a hurry!

Some people say you can't hurry love—well, starting in August, look out for another selection of fabulous romances that prove that sometimes you can!

THE MILLION-DOLLAR MARRIAGE by Eva Rutland—
August 1998

BRIDE BY DAY by Rebecca Winters—
September 1998

READY-MADE BRIDE by Janelle Denison—
December 1998

Who says you can't hurry love?

Available wherever Harlequin books are sold.

HARLEQUIN®
Makes any time special ™